9780872233973

God save the players from people like Donald Ellis who stole the Baltimore Colts' football during the middle of the game!

. . . from Detroit Shirley, the ultimate fan, who will do *anything* to satisfy an athlete.

. . . from Jerry Cusimano who throws octopi onto the ice at hockey games.

. . . from a Montreal fan who has a season ticket for his duck.

. . . from Larry Stakenas, a Chicago Bear fan, who dove out of the stands after a football and landed in a tuba.

GOD SAVE THE PLAYERS

NEIL OFFEN

PLAYBOY PRESS

GOD SAVE THE PLAYERS

Front and back cover photos by Bill Arsenault
Cover and book design by Robert Steven Pawlak

Copyright © 1974 by Neil Offen. All rights reserved.

No part of this book may be reproduced, stored in a retrieval system or transmitted in any form by an electronic, mechanical, photocopying recording means or otherwise without prior written permission of the author.

Published simultaneously in the United States and Canada by Playboy Press, Chicago, Illinois. Printed in the United States of America.

Playboy Press hardcover edition published 1974.
Playboy Press softcover edition published 1975.

PLAYBOY and the Rabbit Head design are trademarks of Playboy, 919 North Michigan Avenue, Chicago, Illinois 60611 (U.S.A.), Reg. U.S. Pat. Off., marca registrada, marque déposée.

This book is available at discounts in quantity lots for industrial or sales-promotional use. For details, write our Special Projects Agency: The Benjamin Company, Inc., 485 Madison Avenue, New York, New York 10022.

FOR CAROL

CONTENTS

Preface 9

1. The Word Is Short for "Fanatic" 16
2. Call Me Loudy 28
3. A Fan Isn't Born: The Story of Creation 42
4. Fanning the Flames: You and the Eye 57
5. Alex and Bill 70
6. The Voice of the People 77
7. Chris, and Henry, Too 86
8. The Craziest Ones of All: Hilda, Shorty and Other Bummers 99
9. Richard Nixon, Ol' Number Twelve 116

10. Who's Plain? What's Average? 130

11. Giving Their All: Violence and the Fan 142

12. Giving Their All: Sex and the Fan 154

13. The Natives Are Restless 166

14. Over There 180

15. The Question Is Why 193

16. On the Inside 208

PREFACE

This is a book about fans, which means it's about you and me, your cousin Egbert, my barber Salvatore. It's about the guy who you wouldn't dare call on Monday nights because of the football games, and the guy with the air horn who is always sitting behind you, no matter which stadium, what sport. You may even be the guy with the horn.

It's about men and women, children and old-age pensioners, and about all those in between. It's about famous fans and rich fans and fans who are anything but. It's about people we envy and some we might pity. It's about people who broadcast their passions on T-shirts and bumper stickers and about people who deny it all and then sneak into the den to turn the game on.

It is, really, about all of us. I believe that. I believe we are all fans, to some degree, in some sense, for some thing. Not all of us are sports fans, but it is sport that seems to speak to us most clearly, to appeal to us most viscerally, in this society, at this time.

To some of us, sports is life, the magic elixir that nourishes while the rest of the world drains. I know of a doctor (who did not want to talk about it for this book) who was told he was suffering from leukemia. He wasn't going to die immediately, but he was going to have to live with the knowledge of a disease that made death something more than abstract. He felt he couldn't live with this knowledge. The fear and anxiety were so great he was going to commit suicide. Then he became involved in the fortunes of a professional basketball team. The team started to have great success and the doctor decided against suicide. He decided—because of the way men unknown to him shoot and pass a round ball—that he was going to live.

To some of us, sport is but one of a panoply of interests. It's an entertainment, good clean fun, momentary exhilaration. It gives us transitory release. When our team wins, there is a warm feeling, something like a minor vindication. We do care, but if our team loses, we are not left desolated.

To others, sport is remote, the playground of children and childlike adults. They dismiss sport, feel superior to it, or do not consider it at all. Yet, every so often, they too are moved, uplifted, changed through sport. When the New York Mets won it all in 1969 it was a transcendent event, much more than just baseball or just sports. My mother, who has always said she'll understand baseball when they start to play it in Yiddish, was excited by that summer. She didn't know what was happening, exactly, but she knew it was something important, and something good.

Like millions of others—who might or might not consider themselves fans—she was enthralled. The cosmic underdog was breaking through. She was not concerned with the mechanics of the hit-and-run play, but she was interested. Sport moves us not so much through grace and skill and the qualities inherent in the games, but through the qualities we project onto them. We see our worlds and we see ourselves—courageous, daring, stalwart. We identify, not with what we are but with what we would like to be, how we would like to live. We look to see how we would react under pressure, how we would come from behind, how we would stay on top, what we would do on the bottom.

PREFACE 11

There is a theory, quite prevalent among pseudoanalysts and glib broadcasters, that sports is a microcosm of life. It isn't. Sports is life to the nth degree. It is life in extremis; every season you are born and you die; every game, every 48 minutes or nine innings, you win and you lose. Every play encompasses an eternity.

Sports is a world speeded up and a world of absolutes. There is good and bad, black and white, right and wrong. It's not gray and tentative like the real world. And in the real world there aren't 50,000 voices cheering us on if we do a good job cleaning the sidewalks.

No, sport is not a microcosm of life. It is hyperlife under glass. It can't show us ourselves, our country, our world in detail. Instead of some diorama of life, it is a repository. It's like a Rorschach test, an ambiguous inkblot that takes whatever form we make of it. We look at that inkblot and we see our needs, hopes and problems. Sport uncovers us. What we bring to it, how we react to it, tells us something about ourselves. Some of us throw bottles, some offer ourselves sexually, some fight and some cry about these games.

At the stadium or in front of the tube we let down the bars. Sports are our passions, and when we are passionate we are defenseless, unfettered by considerations of manners or family or society. This is a book about us, even if we don't recognize ourselves.

This is a book about fans, but not all fans. If it were about all fans, just in the United States, there would be something like 80 million chapters. My editor, Bill Adler, tells me that the copyreaders would be upset. Not to mention the printers.

This is not, therefore, a definitive book. I know there must be someone out in Milwaukee who's been to every demolition derby since 1938. Maybe you know a kid in San Diego who has written fan letters to every member of the Rumanian Davis Cup Team. And how about the lady in Keokuk who redid her kitchen so it would resemble a football? We've all heard of this or that magnificently obsessed fan, the greatest fan in the world, "superfan." Why isn't he in the book?

I offer my apologies. My regrets, Mr. Milwaukee, Master San Diego, Ms. Keokuk. There just wasn't enough room. I make no claims that the fans who are included are the greatest fans, the most dedicated, the most super "superfans." They are here because I thought they were interesting. I also believe they are perhaps a little bit representative of fans in general.

I have concentrated mostly on professional sports. This was only partly arbitrary. While there are people who, for various reasons, live and die every season with a college team, most college fans are captive fans, either through attendance at the school or regional chauvinism. If you're a student at Ohio State, you march in the pep rallies, stoke the bonfires, cheer the effigy-hangings. Then, after four years, you move on, and your fanaticism becomes attenuated.

In other amateur sports the focus is usually on the individual, so there isn't very much continuity for the fan. When a Mark Spitz abandons competitive swimming in order to swim in money, the intensity and commitment of the fan must necessarily lessen. With the professionals, the continuity is there and commitment is long-term.

Specifically, I have tried to deal with the fans of the professional teams, and in this country that means baseball, football and, to slightly lesser degrees, basketball and hockey. No affront is intended to followers of the roller derby, or bowling, or soccer. But our national passions are the big

PREFACE 13

four, and I'm very passion-oriented.

I have tried not to concentrate on any particular geographic areas. The people and incidents described come from all over. Admittedly, there is a lot about New York and its environs, but it was coincidental. I happen to live in New York.

I have also concentrated mostly on modern fans. I know there were many fascinating fans who did marvelous things back in the Twenties and Thirties, but I wanted to be able to speak to the fans, to ask them why. Besides, I think fans have changed somewhat, and what they were like back in the Twenties might not be entirely relevant now.

In trying to make the book representative rather than encyclopedic, I have probably not dealt with some topics that are of interest to fans. There is, alas, nothing coming up about religion and the fan, or the eating habits of the fan. At least I don't think there is.

Finally, this is not intended to be an erudite treatise on something like "the myth of the modern-day sports fan," just a book about some people.

And for helping me do it, I'd like to mention some people. Without them, there would not have been a book. Thank you, Ernie Accorsi, Marty Appel, Red Barber, John Bell, Frank Blauschild, Hal Bock, Larry Bortstein, Irv Brodsky, Bill Brown, Don Casey, Fred Claire, Jim Dunlop, Gerald Eskenazi, Charlie Feeney, Stan Fischler, Pat Graber, John Halligan, Tommy Holmes, Art Keefe, Henry Kellerman, Bernie Kirsch, Jack Lang, Jack Letheren, Pat Mason, Lee Meade, Tom Mee, Clara Mendiola, Hal Middlesworth, Jim O'Brien, Joyce Pruett, Rick Pearson, Dominic Piledggi, Joe Reichler, Don Ruck, Tom Seppy, Norman Smith, George Solomon, Larry Shenk, Frank Van Riper, Bill

14 PREFACE

Veeck, Jim Wergeles, Matt Winick, Bob Wolff, Bob Woolf, Jerry Wynn, Bob Wirz, Vic Ziegel, the New York Public Library, all the people named elsewhere in the book, my trusty ten-dollar Royal upright, and, of course, Carol.

NEIL OFFEN

**To be able to fill leisure intelligently
is the last product of civilization.**
—BERTRAND RUSSELL

Sports is life.
—VINCE LOMBARDI

THE WORD IS SHORT FOR "FANATIC"

1

These are fans:

Edwin A. Lowenthal, a 71-year-old retired industrialist from Evansville, Indiana. Mr. Lowenthal attended each and every World Series game from 1947 through 1966. He saw his first World Series game in 1916. From 1934 until 1966 he missed but five Series games. "Some people want to be millionaires," he said in 1966, "but I always wanted to see World Series games."

Larry Stakenas, a 41-year-old cost estimator from Chicago. Stakenas, a Chicago Bear fan, has a seat in the end zone. "One of my dreams is to get a ball, any kind of ball," he says. Once, after a point-after touchdown, the football came nearby and Stakenas dove over the wall—and right into a tuba.

Larry Loebbers, a farmer in Union, Kentucky, 31 years old when Cincinnati's Crosley Field was being torn down. "I went down to the Crosley to buy two seats for my recreation room. It was a cold day in January and nobody was there to buy the stuff, and, well, one thing just led to another." Loebbers bought both Crosley Field dugouts, the interiors of the clubhouses, the bullpens, the foul poles, the scoreboard, the left-field wall with the advertisements intact, 400 grandstand seats, a popcorn stand, a ticket booth and all the Crosley Field signs.

Two middle-aged men, sitting in a bar in Pittsburgh, testing each other on baseball trivia.

THE WORD IS SHORT FOR "FANATIC" 17

MAN NO. 1: Who led the American League in balks in 1950?
NO. 2: Vic Raschi.
NO. 1: Okay, who holds the record for most base hits in a season?
NO. 2: George Sisler.
NO. 1: All right, all right. Here's one. Who was the catcher for the Cincinnati Reds who committed suicide in 1939?
NO. 2: Wally Hershberger.
NO. 1: Okay, quick, what was he batting when he died?

Lou SanGiovanni, of Los Angeles, a seller of attaché-case telephones. Although he lives in California, Mr. SanGiovanni's heart still belongs to the New York Giants football team, the team he grew up with. When the Giants play and are not on nationwide television, Mr. SanGiovanni calls his mother in Middlesex, New Jersey. After exchanging pleasantries, she turns on the TV set, turns up the volume, puts the phone next to the set and closes the door behind her, leaving her son alone with his Giants. "Expensive?" SanGiovanni laughs. "Nah, maybe fifty, sixty bucks a game. Heck, if I went to the game, what with tickets and dinner and like that, it'd be just as expensive, wouldn't it?" If it's a particularly important Giant game, SanGiovanni will call his mother early so he can get the pregame show.

Valdis Slakans, a factory worker from Galveston, Texas. Slakans is a Detroit Lion fan although he has never seen the Lions play in person, nor has he ever been to Detroit. On Sundays Slakans goes to the games of the Houston Oilers, his local team, wearing a windbreaker in Lions colors and carrying a Lions banner over his shoulder. He sits down in an uncrowded section, takes out his beer, places his short-wave radio in front of him and points the antenna in the direction of Michigan. Then he puts up his sign saying "V.J.

18 GOD SAVE THE PLAYERS

Slakans, World's Greatest DEE-troit Lion Fan." Slakans explains that he does his rooting at a game between two teams he cares nothing about rather than rooting at home, "because I like the atmosphere."

A Montreal resident, name and profession unknown. One afternoon he walked into Jarry Parc to see his Expos play, with a duck perched on his shoulder. An usher told him that no pets were allowed and the duck would have to go. The man dug into his pocket and produced a season ticket for the duck.

Robert Emmett Thornton, B-12151, and John Severnson Watson, B-11037, of San Quentin, California. For Thornton, who lives on death row, and for Severnson, who has a life sentence, being fans—via television, naturally—is what keeps them going. "The pro pigskin parade is taken so seriously here," Watson reports, "that a Raquel Welch movie comes out a poor second to Merlin Olsen and Deacon Jones."

Diana Deis, an 18-year-old student from Milwaukee. During the summer of 1973 Ms. Deis spent over 18 hours a day for over two months atop a 40-foot tower while she waited for the Milwaukee Brewers to win seven games in a row. She waited in vain. She finally ended her vigil because she had contracted pneumonia.

Bill Caughtey and Caryl Meyer, of Minneapolis. On November 7, 1971, they were married in the parking lot outside Metropolitan Stadium before the Minnesota Vikings played the San Francisco 49ers. "I never thought it would be like this when I was a little girl thinking about getting married," the bride said.

THE WORD IS SHORT FOR "FANATIC" 19

Pete Adelis, known as "Leather Lung Pete" or "The Iron Lung of Shibe Park," employed by an advertising agency, of Philadelphia. Twenty-five years ago Pete Adelis was the voice of Philadelphia—the heckling voice. He was six feet tall, weighed 260 pounds and wore a size 52 suit. His voice was larger than his waist. Adelis considered himself—and the As and Phils agreed—"a scientific heckler." The As used to take him on the road with the team, so he could bother the other clubs home and away. The Yankees were so impressed with his heckling and his voice that they brought him up to New York to root against the Cleveland Indians. One game, at Ebbets Field, Adelis was heckling Brooklyn's Billy Herman. This was the day that Arkie Vaughn, one of Herman's closest baseball buddies, had drowned. Adelis boomed out: "Herman, the wrong guy drowned." Herman seriously attempted to kill Adelis. He wasn't successful, but did succeed in getting Adelis banned for life from Ebbets Field.

John R. Kirwan, Jr., a motel manager from Somerset, New Jersey. Kirwan has a collection of over 900 autographed baseballs, starting with a ball autographed by the 1927 Yankees. Among the other balls Kirwan has is one with the autographs of Mrs. Rogers Hornsby, Mrs. Babe Ruth, Mrs. Lou Gehrig, Mrs. Mickey Cochrane and Mrs. Eppa Jeppa Rixey. He also has a ball autographed by the wife of Roy Campanella, who was authorized by her paralyzed husband to sign his name. Kirwan always carries a ball bag around with him, since he never knows when he might gain a signature.

Pete Cusimano, a manager of a coffee selling company, in Detroit. Pete Cusimano throws octopi. It started during the 1952 Stanley Cup playoffs.

20 GOD SAVE THE PLAYERS

Pete and his brother Jerry were fervent Red Wing fans and wanted to do something to propel their team onward. The team had already won seven straight playoff games and the brothers sought out an appropriate symbol.

"My dad was in the fish and poultry business," Pete says, "and my brother and me helped him and often after work, we'd go to the Red Wing games. Anyway, before the eighth game in 1952, my brother suggested, 'Why don't we throw an octopus on the ice for good luck? It's got eight legs and that might be a good omen for eight straight wins.'"

On April 15, 1952, Jerry Cusimano threw his first octopus onto the ice of the Detroit Olympia. The octopus weighed about three pounds, was partially boiled to turn it a deep crimson color and was quite sticky. It also smelled a lot. "You ever smelt a half-boiled octopus?" Pete asks. "It ain't exactly Chanel No. 5, y'know."

Since that first pitch, Pete Cusimano threw an octopus at least once in every Detroit playoff series for the next 15 years. "It's not exactly cherry custard," Pete Cusimano says. "You should see how the referees jump."

A Denver, Colorado, resident, name withheld by the police. The man had been despondent over a Denver Bronco loss to the Chicago Bears. He was so despondent he tried to kill himself, the police reported. He shot himself in the head, but the wound was not fatal. The man had written a note before firing the gun: "I have been a Broncos fan since the Broncos were first organized and I can't take their fumbling anymore."

These are fans. The simple, uncluttered word doesn't seem to do them justice. It doesn't convey the passion, the loonyness, the intensity, the love, the hate, the dependence, the extremes, the variety, the gradations. Its inadequacy stems from the word's background, a tawdry tale. Originally, of course, it was short for "fanatic"—"a person with an extreme and unreasoning enthusiasm or zeal."

There's the rub. It's that "extreme and unreasoning" stuff. The implication is that there's something wrong with it all, something—well, unhealthy about being fanatical about the Denver Broncos. So the word had to be shortened. The *Oxford English Dictionary* reports that the word "fan" first appeared in 1682 and was spelled either fann or phan. At that time it was a "jocular abbreviation of fanatic." Its first known use was in *New News From Bedlam*: "To be her Nurs'd up, loyal Fanns to defame, And damn all dissenters, on purpose for gain." Not too much jocular about that.

The word remained popular in that form until about 1720. From then through the 17th and 18th Centuries the word languished in England. It took the Americans, and the 19th Century, to bring it to flower. *A Dictionary of Slang and Unconventional English* reports that the word first started to appear regularly in the United States around 1899. The definition had been modified slightly: "An enthusiast, originally of sport." At least we were rid of "jocular." The *Dictionary of Americanisms* finds the earliest written reference in 1896: "I'm going to be the worst fan in the whole bunch."

No reference work seems sure exactly who originated the word, if any one individual did. Perhaps it was a headline writer unable to fit "fanatic" in. Nevertheless, the bastard word gained quick acceptance. The English reaccepted it circa 1914. By 1930 the word was considered colloquial, which meant that the headline writer didn't have to explain it to his editor anymore. The word was now used throughout the world as the definitive way to describe *those* people. It was immensely translatable. Spanish-speaking people perhaps translated it best. They started to call them *los fanaticos*.

But dictionary definitions, even of words that have become colloquial, even if they are translated into other languages, are flat and impersonal. So here are some personal definitions. Being personal, they reflect the perspectives of the individuals. That means they are limited, not inclusive, prejudiced, sometimes even silly. But to the holders of these views, they are the real thing.

Don Ruck, vice-president of the National Hockey League: "A fan is someone who gears his life to a sport, or sports. It's a person who might seem to be nuts to the rest of us, but to himself is just shifting gears."

Dominic Piledggi, former president of the Sports Fans of America: "A fan is an individual who, on a fairly regular basis, pays for a ticket out of his own pocket to attend a sports event."

Ron Swoboda, former major-league baseball player: "I guess it's someone who vicariously needs something and so has taken to a sport to get whatever that is he needs. Actually, to a ballplayer, a fan is part of that mindless mass that inhabits the stands."

Henry Kellerman, psychologist and psychoanalyst: "A fan is an individual who is most likely involved in ambition and achievement considerations. Within that framework, a fan is an individual who uses his projective mechanism on sports to work out some particularized conflicts."

Bill Veeck, former president of several major-league baseball franchises and one racetrack: "A fan is an escapist. A fan's a person who wants to get away from the worry of current ills, whether they are personal ones or society's."

Don Weiss, National Football League executive: "A fan is an individual who is very marketable."

Wilt Chamberlain, professional basketball player and coach: "A fan is an animal."

Dr. Arnold R. Beisser, psychiatrist and the author of *The Madness in Sports:* "The fan is an athlete once removed, an athlete in spirit if not in fact. He is a competitor without the necessity of facing the dangers of competition."

Richard M. Nixon, president, United States of America: "I'm a fan."

There is the possibility, of course, that those highly personalized definitions haven't helped to clarify anything, the parts being something less than the sum of the whole. Which brings us to statistics.

Statistics can't tell us about things like intensity, devotion, pain, sorrow, love, anger. But they can—and in this era of polls and opinion samples do—tell us about scope. They can define for us the perimeters of our affair with sports.

First there are the cumulative statistics, the ones that deal with actual numbers, and therefore actual people, not trends and percentages. For instance, the National Football League, which prides itself on its knowledge of its fans, proudly boasts that in 1972 pro-football fans ate five million hot dogs. That's an indication of something (probably good mustard sales).

In 1972, the last year for which records are available, the total estimated attendance at all sporting events in the United States amounted to 280,000,000. The *Daily Racing Form*, the compiler of the statistics, says that figure includes football, baseball, basketball, horse racing, hockey, auto racing, soccer, greyhound racing, boxing and wrestling. The figure, of course, doesn't mean that there are actually 280,000,000 different sports fans. Some of those 280,000,000 probably went to more than one game and thus were counted at least twice. And just because a person went to a game doesn't mean he is a fan, by anyone's definition. If he went just because "All in the Family" was showing reruns that night or because the movie house was charging five dollars to see *Last Tango in Paris*, he shouldn't count. The import of the 280,000,000 is further lessened by the fact that the leading sport, in terms of attendance, was horse racing with 74,015,395. Presumably though, some of them cared little about horses or racing, but went because they might have wanted to win some money.

Still, 280,000,000—and 43,025,559 for football; 38,896,479 for baseball; 34,441,704 for basketball, etc.—are impressive numbers. It shows that we are not alone.

Now for some analytical statistics, the ones that deal with trends, with the whys and the whos.

In January 1972 Louis Harris and Associates revealed the results of the most extensive poll ever made of America's sporting habits and likes. Dealing mostly with the two most popular sports, the survey showed that football, followed by 67 percent of the public, had become America's number one sport, edging baseball by one percent. All other sports trailed badly. The Harris poll went on to show that football fans tended to be richer, better educated, younger and whiter than baseball fans. For instance, of those who made less than $5000 a year, 48 percent said they followed baseball, and 35 percent named football. With those who made $15,000 and over, football leaped to 65 percent, with baseball at 55 percent.

There were two reasons that the poll might be somewhat suspect, however. First, it was taken right before the Super Bowl was played, at the height of the football season and thus months away from baseball. Second, the poll was commissioned by the National Football League.

Since sports now understands that it is big business, the owners and corporate managers of these enterprises are very much influenced by Madison Avenue techniques these days. They keep hiring firms to make "consumer surveys," so they can find out who their fans are, what they want, what they'll take instead. A few examples, and a few statistics, too:

The National Hockey League hired a research firm named Hanan & Son of New York. This is what the National Hockey League got back for its money: 74 percent of hockey-game attenders own a color television set; 90 percent carry life-insurance policies; 62 percent live in a suburban or rural area; 13 percent have received a postgraduate degree; 17 percent are between the ages of 18 and 24.

The NFL's own survey, on the other hand, found that 52 percent of their typical fans are professional, management and executive types; 74 percent drink liquor, with scotch, bourbon and vodka favored; 75 percent have no bank loans other than mortgages; 82 percent entertain at home at least once a month.

On a somewhat smaller scale, students at Emory University in Georgia conducted a consumer survey for the Atlanta Braves. Among their findings was that 11.8 percent of the Braves fans are over 50 years of age; 22.1 percent come from families of over four people; 31.7 percent have incomes over $20,000; 30.9 percent are single.

These surveys were, for the most part, conducted at the ball parks and arenas. So they are by definition limited. You don't have to attend the game to be a fan, just like you don't have to get on the scale to know you're fat.

Which brings us to another kind of survey: television ratings. The A. C. Nielsen Company, which surveys the tube by plugging into 1200 homes across the country, has estimated, for instance, that 80 million people watched the Miami-Washington Super Bowl in 1973, the largest audience ever for television. Nielsen has also claimed that the World Series of 1973 was watched by 60 million people and the National Basketball Asscciation play-offs were watched by 30 million.

Still, those 1200 households, even combined with the five million frankfurter eaters, miss a lot of the true fans out there. No survey tells us anything about the ten-year-old who imagines himself to be Joe Namath. Or the 16-year-old who sends love letters to Johnny Bench. Neither of them may go to any games, and maybe they don't even watch on television. Maybe that five-foot ten-inch kid trying to touch the rim in the schoolyard doesn't even *have* a television set. And the corporate executive who goes to every Laker game and watches all the Rams games on the tube, maybe he's not a fan at all, even though he is one of the 41 percent who has only a mortgage. If he goes just because he believes it's fashionable to go, is he a fan? If he goes just because his son is interested, is he a fan?

Another possible measure of the dimensions of fandom might be the dollar sign: how many shinguards, red-white-and-blue basketballs and Bobby Orr hockey skates are sold in sporting-goods stores. After the Saint Louis Blues hockey team was created in 1967, hockey equipment outsold all other sports equipment in area stores the next year. Did that mean there were more hockey fans than baseball fans in Saint Louis in 1968?

Maybe you can measure by the autographed balls, the "No. 32" pajamas and by all the mustaches young men grew after Mark Spitz won seven gold medals in the Olympics.

Another yardstick might be the amount of damage caused by the riots and near-riots that happened in New York, Pittsburgh, Detroit, Montreal, Boston, Miami, *et al*, after teams from those cities won championships.

And maybe you can't measure it at all. Maybe you can't define being a fan in words, or statistics or dollars spent or seats occupied.

Being a fan is something very personal. It's caring, and how do you measure caring? It's collecting autographed baseballs and wanting to collect point-after-touchdown footballs. It's going to every game. It's sitting up all night in the bar talking Mantle-Mays and it's reading every box score in the newspaper. It's making long-distance calls to get the away game play-by-play. It's getting into fights over the merits of a coach and it's jumping over the rail to fight the coach. It's being moved by grace and courage and being repelled by mediocrity and boredom. It's craving excitement and remembering more peaceful times. It's needs and desires and voids and fulfillment. It's problems and the answers to problems.

Caring. The *Oxford English Dictionary* doesn't say anything about that. Neither does Louis Harris.

CALL ME LOUDY
2

A NEW YEAR, A NEW START
August 4

Here we go, team, in '73, how will we do?
   We'll have to wait and see.
We're practically new, right down the line,
   But with our vets, we'll do just fine.
We're starting anew, and a job we must do,
   And maybe, just maybe, we'll surprise a few.
It's a long road ahead, and it *will* be tough,
   But we'll show them all, that we have the stuff.
      GO COLTS!
            —Hurst "Loudy" Loudenslager

It's a trim little development on the outskirts of Baltimore. The houses are all one-family, level buildings with brick frontings and neatly tended postcard-size lawns. You could be on one winding street and think you were on another.

House after house after house. Except this one. On the lawn of this one rises a 30-foot white flagpole, and floating in the breeze at the top of the flagpole is a blue flag with white lettering: COLTS. This is Loudy Loudenslager's house.

There is no indication on the main floor of the house that this is the home of the number-one Baltimore Colt football fan in the entire world. Nothing except, perhaps, the embroidered blue and white (Colt colors) pillow on the couch, which says "Colts" and " '58–'59," a championship year. It is downstairs, in the basement den, that this man's passion is on display. On the walls along the stairway are all the Colt team pictures since 1947, carefully framed and protected by glass. The den itself is paneled in knotty pine and Colt memorabilia. Johnny Unitas's uniform is framed and hung on the wall. Gino Marchetti's uniform is on the wall as are uniforms of other illustrious Colts. There is Don Shinnick's knee brace, carefully hung. On a pedestal in front of the wall rests Lou Michaels's kicking shoe. "Colt Corral" pennants, insignias of the largest organized sports fan club in the country, are all over. Bronzed footballs and helmets are scattered throughout the fairly small room. Everywhere you look there are Colt ashtrays and Colt banners and Colt letters and Colt newspaper stories. "There are also cartons and cartons of stuff that I just don't have anywhere to put," Loudy Loudenslager says. "I guess I'm just going to have to enlarge this room or something."

Loudy Loudenslager ("I hate to be called Hurst") is 60 years of age, short and round. His hair is brown and receding, his face oval and friendly. He is a career man in the National Guard, a sergeant, and next year, he thinks, he will retire. He is married to a prim, tasteful-looking woman named Flo. He is the father of two children, both grown and married. He is a grandfather. He has lived in Baltimore all his life and since 1947 he has been devoted to the Baltimore Colts football team.

"After family, religion and flag and country," he says, and he says it tenderly, not bombastically, "the most important thing in the world to me is the Colts."

WE'RE JUST BEGINNING
August 11

O'Kay, Team, game No. 1 is past,
    Losing is something we won't let last,

We now have played one of the best,
   And, all in all, we stood the test.
Together with teamwork, hitting and more desire,
   We'll come along, and catch on fire.
Then we'll go right on from there,
   And we will start to climb the stairs.

"I first got involved the very first game in 1947 that we had a football team. There were about twelve thousand fans I guess out there that first time. I hadn't really been a fan before, but it was the first game, and I thought, why not, I'll go out there, see what it's all about. From that very first game, really, I loved it.

"Each succeeding game that I went to, I liked it so much more so I thought it would be nice to get to know the guys. You know, it is your team. I thought it would be nice to get to know them. So I'd start down to the dressing room at the end of the game, wait for them to come out. I'd say 'very nice game,' 'way to go,' or something like that. I got to know their names—and they got to know mine. That was you know, '48, '49 and '50. Then they took the team out of town and they didn't come back until 1953. Me and this friend of mine, we were two of the first to put our money down to bring the team back, to put out for season tickets. It started from there. You know, it's something you just do . . . it just happens I guess. Each game I'd go down to the dressing room and stay in there, wait for them to come out, hit them on the tail, say 'nice game, Don, Bob, Joe' or whatever. And from there on, I just kept on doing it, getting more and more involved."

Loudy is sitting comfortably on the couch in the basement. He has the stereo playing, very softly. It's playing something mildly pop, perhaps Mantovani. Loudy's wife Flo is upstairs in the kitchen. Otherwise, the house, the neighborhood, perhaps the whole world, is perfectly quiet, perfectly still. It's a very calm, relaxed, comfortable world. Loudy Loudenslager has all he wants in the world around him, and so he is very content. He doesn't seem possessed by his passion for the Colts, feverish about it. In his comfortable world he feels no need to proselytize, convince, argue. This is, he is saying, how he is. And it is the way he wants to be.

WE'RE COMING ALONG
August 18

Slowly but surely we're coming on,
 We're doing our best to get the job done.
We did much better in game No. 2,
 When we play the Lions, we'll improve more too.
We'll show them all, that we came to play,
 We're gonna get better, day by day.
So, let's rock 'em and sock 'em and give 'em hell,
 We're coming along, and we're gonna jell.

In 1957 the involvement started to grow even larger for Loudy Loudenslager. He heard that someone had started a Colts Corral, an organized fan club for the team. He talked the idea over with some of his buddies in the National Guard, Colt fans all. Together with their wives, they started Colts Corral Number Two. There are now 23 Corrals. For ten years Loudy has been secretary of the Corral Council. "Ever since 1957," he says, "I've been completely wrapped up in it."

Loudy talks of the Corrals as some would talk of their church, or others their consciousness-raising group. "Each year each Corral would have its affairs, honoring players. Each one would think of its own title to honor a player: most outstanding player, most dedicated player, Colt wife of the year, whatever. You know, a few months ago, a fellow in Washington called me and asked me for some advice because they were interested in forming some Redskin Tee Pees. I said, 'Fine, why don't you drop over to our next council meeting, the presidents of all the Corrals would be there and we'll talk with you and maybe you could get some ideas. We'll give you the bylaws, constitution, everything you'll need to know.' Do you know that now they already have two Tee Pees? And two more are forming? Of course, the Redskins don't help their Tee Pees at all, they just let them use the name. But with the Colt organization you're part of the family, it's as simple as that. But with the Redskins, it's good. What the heck, I'm glad to see it. I'm glad to see that people care."

Loudy Loudenslager cares. Being a member of a Corral or even being the secretary of the Corral Council, wasn't caring enough. That same year, 1957, he started going down to Baltimore's Friendship Airport to see the team off when they left to play a road game.

"I was just going down there at first to say hi. It wasn't the way it is today."

CONGRATULATIONS, TEAM
August 25

We've won No. 1, and that's a fact,
 From now on, team, we're in the act.
We did it *together*, just as one,
 From here on out, we'll get the job done.
We're coming along more, each day,
 As each game passes, we'll be on our way.
So stick in there, team, keep plugging away,
 We'll move right up, and have our day.

The way it is today started for Loudy in 1960. The Colts had been champions the previous two seasons and when they left the airport, or returned

CALL ME LOUDY 33

to the airport, particularly from one of their victories, there were usually hundreds there, reveling in it. Then in '60 the Colts had a bad season, and the crowds seeing them off and welcoming them home dwindled. "There was nobody, honestly, nobody," Loudy remembers. He is a man of stringent loyalties, a patriotic man who believes in his church, his country, his team right or wrong. He was very personally offended by the absence of the crowds.

"Wait a minute. Waaait a minute, I thought. There's got to be something wrong with this. It really disturbed me." He was not angry at the front-runners, not bitter with his fellow fans, but disturbed for the players, for his friends. "I wrote an article to the newspaper—which I have framed up there on the wall—about how is it too much to get off your butt now, after we've had two championships and, well, you know, that kind of thing.

"Well, about this time, this long-playing record came out with all the fight songs of all the teams in the NFL, and I bought it and thought, heck, goddammit, I don't know if anyone's ever done it or not, but what's wrong with taking this Colt fight song, taking it down to the airport when the team leaves, and hitting 'em with it? When they're getting on the airplane, right?

"So I started, and right away everybody thought what the hell's going on? I guess they thought I was a little crazy. In fact, it was pretty funny. The first time I went and did it, I'll never forget this guy. He was a United Airlines guy, one of the people who took the passengers on the plane. Well, I went down with this little portable record player, and I went right up to where the guys get on the plane and I put it right down. I started to set it up, you know, plugged it into their wall, and this guy comes over and says, 'What are you doing? What are you *doing?*'

" 'What am I doin'? What do you *think* I'm doing? It's obvious. I'm setting up a record player, plugging it into the wall. I got the Colt fight song here,' I tell him, 'and I thought it would be nice to play the team off.'

" 'Ohhh, you can't do that, you can't do that. Oooohhh,' he says to me. 'We got a million-dollar airplane. We can't have you out here doing this.' I told him, 'I don't want your million-dollar airplane. I only want to play the record.' Oh, he was highly disturbed. He said he'd have to go upstairs and check, and he did, and I guess someone must've told him to leave the nut alone. And he did. And that was the first time I did it."

WE'LL DO IT IN DENVER
September 8

We'll do it in Denver, because we must,
   In each other we'll put our trust.
Let's Rock 'em and Sock 'em and play 'em tough,
   If we do this, team, it will be enough.
We'll then be ready for game No. 1
   And surprise one and all before we're done.

Loudy doesn't know exactly, but he guesses he's been to the airport, to wave good-bye to the Colts or to pat them on their backs when they return, something over 350 times. Every time he has been there, he has taken with him the weatherbeaten little record player that is sitting over there on a table. He says he's gonna have to get a new one soon; this one is going. The players, he says, are used to him now and used to hearing the Colt fight song when they leave and when they return. They expect it. But that first time—well, Loudy remembers, maybe they did think it was a little odd.

"That first time, they were surprised, naturally. Like, 'Hey, what's going on? Here's the Colt fight song.' They never had heard anything like that before. They were surprised, and then there were the needles. You know, one of the great things I've gotten out of all this is the needles, the ribbing. But I know that they wouldn't bother to needle me if they didn't care. It means something. It's not a needle that I don't like you. It makes it all worthwhile."

Loudy hunches forward, about to tell a story he relishes, a story that anyone would relish: righteous indignation being rewarded.

He had been playing the fight song at the airport for about five years. Then one night the players were arriving, the record player was all set and the song was about to play, when "This airport policeman came down the stairs and asked me what am I doin'. I've only been doing it for five years. Every game, you know. Well, he says, 'I'm sorry, but you can't do this. You're going to have to leave.' And I was shocked. I'd been doing this for five years. I said wait a minute. He said forget it, close it up and move out of here. I was really upset.

"Well, I thought, you're just not going to defeat me. So I went out to where the cars were parked, and you could plug the record player into the fence out there and that's what I did. And I played it out there."

Loudy smacks his lips. This is the climax. "Well, the next day, a guy I know who works at the airport, he tells me, 'You know, Loudy, you really stirred up a hornet's nest out there last night.' 'What do you mean *I* stirred up a hornet's nest?' Well, he tells me, the players get off the plane and they don't see me and they ask, 'Where's Loudy?' And the guard said he moved him out. They said, 'You did?' Well, my friend tells me, that next morning they held a big meeting at the airport, some of the Colts, the police, the people from United, and they were politely told to leave me alone." Loudy opens his eyes wide. "And they have."

BEST WISHES ON THE SEASON, TEAM
September 16

The training season is over,
   There were games we lost and won,
But we can be in clover before the season is done,
Let's make it one for all, and all for one.
And together we'll be just fine.
   Good Luck, and
"Let's Go You Baltimore Colts!"

Five years after he started playing the fight song, Loudy decided to add an extra fillip to his airport visits. He began writing little poems, with predictions (Colts 17, Steelers 14), on little cards and giving them to the players. "Again, it just started out of the clear blue. One night I thought, just for the heck of it I'll write a little something, to send 'em off with. So I sat down and wrote the first one, and from then on, each game. I got involved, and it just got going."

Loudy writes the poems, adds his predictions, signs each card "Good luck, Loudy" and then has his son, a printer, print them up. For each game, each season, there is a different card. Each time, at the airport, Loudy will give each player, each official, one card. "Oh, usually I'll just say hi, give them the card, pat them on the tail or something."

The only constant in the cards, other than the rhyme scheme, is that he has never predicted a Colt loss. "Oh, no way," he says. "You know, one time Jimmy Orr [a Colt receiver] says to me at the airport, 'Loudy, don't you ever pick us to lose? You know we do lose sometimes.' 'I'll tell you what, Jim,' I said to him. 'I'll pick a losing score for the next ball game, but you give the cards out.' "

Every game he manages to come up with a poem. He has no writer's block. "Oh, I just sit down and write them out. Whatever comes to my mind, I just put it down and it usually works out okay."

When a man has such a magnificent obsession, it is difficult, if not downright impossible, for those closest to him to remain uninvolved. Loudy has his son printing his poems. And for his wife, the quiet, reserved Flo, Loudy has something, too.

Flo, who has been married to Loudy for 36 years, is also a fan. She would have to be. These are not people who pursue separate identities, reach separate levels of consciousness. This is not an open marriage. Their lives are entwined, and entwined around Loudy Loudenslager's interests. Flo goes to as many games with her husband as possible. "The only thing is," Loudy says, "she really hates the cold so she doesn't go to that many when it gets late in the year." Many times she goes to the airport with him. In the early years, the whole family would go. But Flo's involvement then was mostly peripheral.

Then Loudy got this idea. "It was just another idea I had, out of the blue. I never realized then how much it was going to cost me. I really can't remember how it started. I thought, like I said, out of the clear blue, that I wanted to get one of the Colts a birthday cake. And it started out from one person, I don't even remember who. That was about six years ago."

From one person, it grew to everyone connected with the Colts—the players, the coaches, the management, the front office, the people in the ticket office, ex-management, ex-players. On his birthday, every person associated with the Colts received a birthday cake with a candle in it, and a card, from Loudy Loudenslager. All year long, in season, out of season. "Originally they were bought cakes, at four, four and a half dollars apiece. And a card, too. I did it that way for about three years. But like I said, it got to be pretty expensive. I wasn't realizing that it was all adding up. You know, in the course of a year, it was way over forty cakes. It got to be pretty expensive."

Flo was the one who pointed that out to Loudy. Better than that, she illustrated it for him. "You see, one night we had a black-walnut cake that Flo had made for dinner, and I said, 'Hey, instead of me spending four and a half or five bucks for a cake, how about, would you make the cakes?' So she said yes. She's gotta be one in a million. There couldn't be another one like her, really. She said yes. And boy, that black-walnut cake is really something. When I walk into the clubhouse and give the cake to whoever's having the birthday, well, it takes, I bet you, all of forty-five seconds for that cake to disappear. They love her black-walnut cake."

WE'RE COMING ALONG
October 7

More and more we're coming around,
We'll stick together, we won't let each other down.
It's a long, long way up ahead,
But we won't roll over and we won't play dead.
We'll keep right on working for the day
When we'll get in front to stay.
We'll keep on fighting and let 'em all know
That we'll stick right in there and keep on the go.

Dusk is coming, and bringing with it a chill. Outside, a breeze has turned into a wind and is whipping the Colts flag into furls. The flag is at half-mast because the Colts had lost the weekend before. Some of Loudy's neighbors—he doesn't know which—respectfully lowered the flag.

Inside, it is insulated. President Nixon is wallowing, still, in Watergate this weekend. Automobile drivers are being told that gasoline may be rationed this weekend. The Israelis and the Egyptians are preparing to start negotiations. Phnom Penh, Cambodia, is being bombed again this weekend. But inside, it is insulated.

"One," Loudy Loudenslager is saying, "I've missed just one game since the Colts started playing. And since I started going to the airport, I've missed that just once, too. Both happened when I had a heart attack. Actually, it was a heart seizure. I tell you, when the doctor told me I couldn't go to the game I could have killed myself."

He takes care of himself now, making sure not to scream too much at the game, not jumping up too much—unless, of course, the Colts score. But there are certain limits, certain things a man must do if he is to be his own man. "I believe in doing my own thing," Loudy Loudenslager, the career National Guard man, says. "I believe in everybody doing their own thing."

So, if he has to, he gets up at three or four in the morning to go down to the airport, in the rain, the sleet, the cold. If he is on vacation and the Colts are playing, he'll drive the hundreds of miles for the game. A man must listen to the world, within limits. After those limits, he must listen to himself.

"Sure it's an obsession. If you get up at three

in the morning to meet a football team, of course that's an obsession. But what's wrong with an obsession? How about if you play golf? You get up at four in the morning to go hit a little ball and walk miles and miles to see if it fell into a little hole. Isn't that an obsession?"

He has chosen his own particular obsession and he is content with it. He is not about to dissect it, ravage it, intellectually reject it. Like flag, family and church, it is inviolate.

"Maybe it's my own way of being part of the team. I can't play, but it's my way of being part. It's something—I wish I could explain it—it's just . . ." He sits back, smiling. So he can't explain it, so what? Anyway, it all boils down to a simple equation: "Listen, I've gotten more than I've given. The people, they're good people. You really get to know them and you find out what good people they are. And I'm proud that I've known them. You're darn right I'm proud.

It's something—well, it's something that has pure love in it, you know. It's—you know—heck —listen, if thirty years ago, you'da told me I'd be involved in something like this, I'da never believed it. Heck, everyone has something in their lives that don't belong, don't they?"

STICK IN THERE, TEAM
November 11

Ok, team, things are bad,
    But that's the way it goes.
From here on out we've *really* got to fight,
    And take it to our foes.
Let's pick ourselves up, go on from here,
    And give it all we've got.
And *that* from here on to one and all,
    We'll certainly mean a lot.
Fans and Team, we win or we lose,

But we'll always be with you.
Colts 19   Good Luck
Dolphins 16   "Loudy"
Colts Corral No. 2

In the winter of 1973, Loudy Loudenslager belonged. He was tendered two testimonial dinners. The first was hosted by present Baltimore Colt players and the second by oldtimers like Johnny Unitas and Gino Marchetti. "He always has something kind to say," explained a former Colt.

A FAN ISN'T BORN: THE STORY OF CREATION

3

Loudy Loudenslager's loyalty is unadulterated and unbought. He doesn't need a "pantyhose night" to bring him out to the ball park. He might even be offended by it. But not many teams have Loudy Loudenslagers to depend on to fill their seats and buy their hot dogs. The Washington Senators surely didn't have any.

The management of the lightly patronized Senators, in an effort to get more people into their ball park and to create their own Loudenslagers, did hold a "pantyhose night" at one game. They had, of course, a run on it.

In all sports—particularly baseball, but not exclusively—managements have attempted to create fans and get more people into their buildings by holding: ladies day; puck night; cap day; helmet day; helmet weekend; senior citizens day; retirees day; old-timers day; 'A' students night; back-to-school day; T-shirt day; jersey night; poster day; banner day; orchid night; deodorant night; batting-glove day; ball day; stick night; basketball night; cushion day; Kool-Aid circus day; Burger King day; Ronald McDonald hamburger day; Coca-Cola night; bagel night; Pepsi-Cola night; Mother's Day day; family day; dads-and-sons night; player's family day; camera day; fan-appreciation day; pennant night; college night; teen night; businessman's special night; grand-stand-manager's night; Little League day; shrine night; Hollywood-stars night; prize day; bingo night; ladies night; and maybe a few others.

Sports managements have also tried, in addi-

A FAN ISN'T BORN: THE STORY OF CREATION 43

tion to all the nights and days, a variety of other gimmicks. They've tried scoreboards that explode; zoos in the outfield; automatic rabbit-ball dispensers; Strategic Air Command supersonic jets performing dips; bikinied ball girls; mini-skirted base cleaners; cavorting dolphins; cuddly bassett hounds; toga-clad usherettes; cowboy-hatted usherettes (careful research has yet to uncover any topless or bottomless usherettes). There have also been billboards, booklets, contests, commercials, wildly colored uniforms, wildly colored basketballs, footballs, skates and pucks. As further inducements to become fans, there have been half-time shows, rock bands, magicians, additional games, fashion shows, milking contests, wheelbarrow races, men's fashion shows, autograph booths and assorted cupcakes, free.

In one of the truly classic attempts to create fans, the Milwaukee Brewers baseball team in 1971 had a man known as Bernie Brewer station himself on a small platform above the stadium and live there, completely self-sufficient, for several months. He would stay there, the team advertised, until the Brewers drew 40,000 fans to a game. Apparently the scheme didn't work, because since then the Brewers have had designed and built the "World's Largest Beer Barrel." They've built a chalet above it and connected it to the barrel with a chute so that a new "Bernie Brewer" could slide into a beer stein in front of the barrel after every Brewers home run and victory. While Bernie is sliding, sirens go off, lights flash on the face of the barrel, and then balloons are released as Bernie arrives in the stein.

Just in case that doesn't work, the management has also dressed their ground crew and "Bonnie Brewer," the base-sweeping girl, in lederhosen outfits that come in team colors.

The point of it all, of the nights and days, of the

44 GOD SAVE THE PLAYERS

togas and bands and dolphins, is to get people into the house. The underlying assumption is that fans are not born, they are wheedled, enticed, brought struggling, tempted, drawn, attracted, captivated, titillated, seduced, inveigled. They are created.

Psychologists say fans already have certain inborn qualities which force them, drive them, to become fans. Television people say the tube is the most powerful fan-creating force there is. The commissioners of sports say that fans are fans because——well, because they've always been fans.

It is all true. But just as the child prodigy who can whistle in tune and loves music still has to be taught the notes to play the piano, the fan still has to be nurtured. All those latent tendencies have to be brought out of the closet and the TV den. They have to be focused.

A fan is a specific entity. Just because you like baseball and used to be a pretty good first baseman for the Tenth Street Tigers, that doesn't mean you're going to be a Cleveland Indians baseball fan. *That* specific fan must be created.

Yet, there *are* fans who are not created, who are, in truth, born. Your father has been following the Cleveland Indians ever since he was a child because his father followed the Cleveland Indians. When you were born, instead of putting the silver spoon into your hand, your father placed an Indians pennant. You were named after Lou Boudreau, the Cleveland infielder. Your father made sure your room was wallpapered in Indian batting averages. You were never allowed to wear either red or white socks. And psychologically you felt a deep, almost symbiotic affinity with Al Rosen, the third baseman.

There are fans like that. But as Bill Veeck, probably the greatest sports promoter in the country, says, "As an owner of a team, you are dependent on repeat business. If you break down your attendance figures over a period of time, you will find that on a total attendance of, say, one million, less than 100,000 people are involved. A hundred thousand is a lot more than a hard-core. Those are people you've earned."

The hard-core people like Loudy will come to the games whether management has installed a beer stein or the world's largest wine carafe. The management is not worried about the hard-core. They want the other 90 percent.

Most owners and managers and publicity directors have a very simple answer to how to obtain that 90 percent. Win games. Be successful —that'll bring the people out. Bob Hope, the publicity director of the Atlanta Braves, puts it this way: "Of course, the easiest way to gain fans is to have a winning team on the field. A winning team creates excitement. That's what the people want."

Bill Veeck was president and owner of the Chicago White Sox, the Cleveland Indians and the Saint Louis Browns baseball teams. He has also owned and operated Suffolk Downs Race Track, in addition to being involved with other sports and teams during his promoting career. He once sent a midget up to bat in a major-league game. He is considered a maverick, antiestablishment, a troublemaker. He is considered all these things because he has not sat back and let the fans get away from him.

He is sitting back now in his comfortable living room off a lake on the eastern shore of Maryland. He is chain-smoking and slowly sipping some coffee. He has been in the world of sports for more than half a century. He considers everything he says quite carefully.

"Most owners will say 'all you need is a winning club,'" Veeck says. "Well, that immediately dooms most ball clubs to failure before they start. Sure, historical record will show that over a period of years you can do much better with a winning team. Sure it's better to at least be competitive. That all has to do with identification. If a fan identifies with a team and that team keeps losing, he'll get a little tired of getting his brains beaten in. It's not the team, it's him getting his brains beaten out.

"Baseball, particularly, has been sold on the won-and-lost column. And that's the way fans *have* been made. That's been indoctrinated into the owners. In reality, the game between the fifth and sixth clubs is usually a better game than between the first and sixth clubs. And anyway, except for the record, if the sport has any merit, it shouldn't matter who wins."

Still, as Veeck says, "as long as in people's minds the product is excellence rather than a game, it's always more difficult to sell an inferior product." The idea is to change people's minds. In order to wean them away from the traditional wisdom and the won-lost ethic, first you have to deemphasize winning. "When I had the Saint Louis Browns, who were very mediocre," Veeck remembers, "I used to tell people, very honestly, you better come out because you will never have a chance to see this collection of athletes again. Or, I'd tell them if you have an important decision to make, come out and enjoy the peace and quiet of Sportsman's Park. No one will disturb you. I mean, if you don't have a good club, you can't convince anyone you do. If you're twenty-two and a half games behind the seventh-place team, you can't make people believe you're worldbeaters."

The National Football League, the most successful creator of fans in the last 20 years, has deemphasized winning and sold unpredictability and excitement. It's sold the on-any-given-Sun-

A FAN ISN'T BORN: THE STORY OF CREATION 47

day theory. Anything can happen; any team is capable of beating any other team. It's a good *game*, unpredictable. But pro football is an exception. The traditional wisdom still prevails. Fans want winners. Winners create fans.

The theory is prevalent although it seems to be contradicted by a great amount of evidence. Throughout the early Sixties the New York Yankees were the most successful, winningest team in baseball. But their attendance went down. When the New York Mets, the worst team in baseball, came into operation in 1962, they immediately drew exceptionally well. Baseball's Montreal Expos and hockey's Atlanta Flames each started operations with teams that were among the worst in their respective sports, but still attracted fans. In Boston in the 1950s the Bruins hockey team, in the cellar, always outdrew the Celtics basketball team, in the penthouse. The Baltimore Orioles, over the last few years one of the most artistically successful teams in baseball, with Brooks and Frank Robinson, have never drawn well. The Portland Trailblazers of the NBA, always near the bottom of the league, have always been near the top in gate receipts.

Many of the reasons for these seeming dichotomies, of course, can be found in geographics, demographics, competition and, possibly, even luck. But much of it must also go to conscious, concerted efforts to create fans. The traditional wisdom obviously has changed in some places.

Another piece of that wisdom has been that the game is the thing. The "product" will sell itself. Fans are fans because we have such a great product to offer here. Baseball / football / basketball / hockey / curling / double-kayaking / luge racing is tremendously exciting. Everybody else thinks so, shouldn't you?

48   GOD SAVE THE PLAYERS

"A lot of operators take the position, 'you owe it to us to come out. Our product is so good, you have to come out.' Well, nobody owes you anything," Veeck says.

This emphasis on the product deemphasizes the have-to-win aspect, but creates an inflexibility that is just as harmful. If the people aren't coming, then there must be something wrong with them. There's nothing wrong with us.

"Take baseball, for instance," says Veeck. "Baseball's refused to take any kind of radical moves that would add more offense and excitement to the game, at least until they put in the designated-hitter rule. For fifty years, they kept believing the product was enough. They might raise the mound or alter the strike zone, but they wouldn't essentially tamper with the product. It had worked for them in the past so they thought it was something inviolable."

The traditional wisdom, subdivisions *a* and *b*, has of course been failing. Overall baseball attendance—when you discount the additional number of teams—has been falling for over 20 years. A very small number of teams in the professional basketball leagues are making it at the gate. Football, which up until recently had been the great success story of modern sports, has started experiencing some qualms; practically every game is still sold out, but when Congress invalidated the NFL's blackout rule, a lot of ticket-holding fans become "no-shows."

"The game and the players and even winning isn't enough anymore," Veeck claims. "You're competing with too much for that to be enough anymore."

Don Ruck, the vice-president of the National Hockey League, who came to hockey from advertising, says, "We are not in the sports business, or the ice business. We're in the entertainment business. We're competing against movies and plays and television and going to the pizza parlor to listen to the jukebox. There is only so much disposable income and so much free time that people have. We're in competition for that."

With that in mind, the *new* wisdom of sport —of sport as entertainment—is that sports fans can be created. They must be created. The new realization is Don Ruck saying, "Of course you can create fans anywhere, for any team."

Veeck believes that "If I had a baseball team in New Delhi, India, and they had never heard of baseball, I think I could create fans for the team. I could get them into my building. And once I get them into my building, I figure I can get them back. If I can't get them back, I figure it's my fault, not theirs."

The first thing the promoter must do, "absolutely the first thing," Veeck continues, "is to disseminate news. There has to be dissemination of news of what the game is about. You have to have sufficient coverage over a sufficient period of time to stir up enough interest to get people to go to your particular emporium."

The dissemination of information doesn't have to come through television. It can be word-of-mouth, billboards, anything. "The thing you do, or at least the things I did," Veeck says, "was to go and speak at any crossroads, any town, any place. Any time you can get two people to listen. If there were seven of them, I would play the eighth hand of bridge. That was the way we did it. But I can hardly see Joan Payson [the elderly, aristocratic owner] of the Mets going out to speak to the Elks Club. You do it the way that's most comfortable."

After dissemination of news about the game itself, then, Veeck says, the most important thing is to tell them where and when. "You have to disseminate the news that they are going to play the game. Obviously you can't draw a crowd if nobody knows where to go. Then you get some newspapermen to cover it, and if the people have some fun, they tell other people, and you'll get some stories in the newspapers and it becomes a snowball."

It is important here to understand why people go to games. First, as promoters like Ruck have emphasized, is entertainment. "The sports fan is an escapist," Veeck says. "He wants to be away from his current ills, whether they are his own or society's. He wants entertainment."

There are also generally two other reasons. "It's a vicarious form of excitement," says Veeck. This is where identification and, thus, winning, enter. Nothing can be done by the promoters about that. But people go for social reasons. It is with the entertainment and social aspects that individual initiative pays off.

"It's extremely important to realize," says Veeck, "that people also go to sports events to socialize. Most people if they look in a nightclub and they see no one there, no matter how good the act is, they won't go. We like crowds. We're a gregarious people. So, first, to get crowds, it's important to have crowds, even if that means letting the people in for nothing."

Sports has become social because it is the last of the great levelers. "People from all different backgrounds can talk to each other about sports, and in the same language," Veeck believes. "By being interested in sports, it guarantees that when you talk about it, you won't be rebuffed. The other person will know what you're talking about. Other than sports, the only other time people can freely converse is during disasters. I guess sports is like a hurricane."

To capitalize on this need to socialize, teams

have helped in the creation of fan clubs, booster organizations and the like. The idea is to try and keep the social thing going when the game is not on. Keep the team in the forefront of the frontal lobes. The social aspect is also why the teams hold their family nights and the dad-and-son nights and the ladies days and nights. Going to the game is something all of us can do together. Come on out, watch a few innings, socialize.

Veeck went even further than that. "When we operated the White Sox," he remembers, "I used to sit an inning, inning and a half in every section of the park. Two innings in the bleachers, an inning in each pavilion, lower deck, upper deck. I wanted to get the feel of the people and I wanted them to feel that I was just another guy, not some remote presence. I wanted them to feel like they were coming to my house, not to a ball park."

In all the parks Veeck operated he applied his "checkerboard" theory. If one season's box was sold, he made sure that the one near it was left open for the customers who weren't season subscribers, so they felt they were being treated equally. He also employed his "spotting" theory. Through season-ticket requests, Veeck would find out the professions of his customers. Then he'd sit all the stockbrokers together, all bartenders, all barbers. "If the game was boring, we wanted to make sure they had something to talk about," he explains.

If the game was boring . . . that's how Veeck got involved with other modes of "entertainment." "Our theory was that you have to create some degree of extraneous entertainment. That was the reason for the exploding scoreboards, the bands, the fireworks. I couldn't guarantee that every game was going to be fascinating—or what I considered fascinating. So I would try to provide entertainment so that they would walk away happy even if the club lost. If you lost nineteen to one the fireworks might save you."

Veeck created his entertainments without the advice of market-research people and without the help of consumer surveys. The new way, he feels, is too structured, too formal and too lacking in spontaneity.

"We just tried to keep things happening," he says. "We tried to create an atmosphere." Specific nights for bagels or pantyhose don't, he thinks, have anything to do with atmosphere. They are just isolated incidents.

"I deal in the elements of surprise," he says. "If I operate a ball club again, I will do a lot of things, but I have no reason to tell anybody what they are. My theory was you'd want to come to see what was going to happen next. You don't say come today and you'll see a wire-walker, you just put him on. You have to remember, you're not advertising some other event, you're advertising your sport."

That is the fault Veeck finds with the promotions of today. "I didn't look on the giveaways as the old giving dishes away at the movies during the depression. You were selling the dishes instead of the movie. That's why I reserved the right to do something some nights and other nights nothing. We were selling baseball and all we were trying to do was to create a festive atmosphere.

"If a guy is coming to your game just to get a bat, he's going to get annoyed if you give him a lousy bat. He's going to get annoyed with you and he's not going to come back.

"And having something like pantyhose night. I wouldn't have something like that because that's like having deodorant night. You embarrass people who need large ones. It's also, I think, in bad taste. And anyway, you can't have all sizes."

Veeck, who created ball day and bat day, tried

"a light and kind of gay and casual and fun" approach. But even with his relaxed method, there were problems.

"We had a terrible disaster once in Saint Louis. I was friendly with a guy who was a Teamsters official and he told me of this huge shipment of rubber balls they had, and they were stuck with. I took them and we gave all of them out at a game. That was one of our first ball days. The only trouble was, the first batter hit the ball, the first pitch of the game, and he hits it to right field, just in front of the screen. Just as the ball gets to the screen, here they come. Five hundred balls. Flying out of the stands. They had had no idea which was the real ball. They had to start the game over again.

"Then there was the time in Cleveland where we gave away orchids. We were the first team in the country to give away orchids, long before the supermarkets did at their openings. We did it only because I met this guy in the Biltmore Hotel florist shop who was stuck with his whole labor force and didn't have any market for his orchids. So we got twenty-five thousand of them. Unfortunately, that wasn't enough. We almost had a riot. Everybody wanted their orchids. We started giving out rain checks, but we got into trouble with that, too. We originally said come next ladies day and you'll get them, but we would've started the whole thing over again. So finally I got the women to write down their addresses and had orchids sent to them."

All of Veeck's promotions seem to have started accidentally and then carried through on the wings of a whim. He started bat day because he had bought the stock of a bankrupt bat company. He started fan-appreciation day one year in Cleveland when he decided on the last day of the season to just thank everyone for his 2.3-million attendance for the year. So he let everyone in for nothing. The whole atmosphere was casual, and surprising. "We used to play lucky numbers," he remembers. "You got a number with your seat and if we picked that number we'd give away five thousand cupcakes. It was a wonderful picture to see. What does a guy do with five thousand cupcakes? We delivered them to his house, no matter what the guy said. We just unloaded them." Veeck would also give out two tickets to the next game as a prize if you had the lucky number. In Chicago one year he bought everybody a beer and a Coke on opening day so they could drink a toast to themselves.

The essential question here is: Is the cupcake freak a fan? Can someone turned on by a free orchid develop a lifelong affection for a ball team? Does a free bat win friends and influence people?

"You can't make someone a fan until you get him there, to your building, first. Sure, a guy can be a fan if at first he's only interested in the exploding scoreboard. If you get him there with that, eventually you indoctrinate him.

"In Saint Louis, we set an attendance record with a team that never got out of last place. They were coming to see what crazy things we would do. But they stayed. They had become fans. They had been created."

Times have changed since the days of the St. Louis Browns. So have methods of promotion. The Atlanta Hawks have fired a basketball man as their general manager and hired a promotion-oriented man to replace him. Frequently teams farm out their promotional ventures to ad agencies and market-research facilities. Marketing has taken over the world of sports. The Magnavox company, trying to end a long sales decline, has tied its success to Henry Aaron and home run

A FAN ISN'T BORN: THE STORY OF CREATION 55

number 715. And number 715, which would normally go to the Baseball Hall of Fame, goes on tour amid televisions and stereos. Secretariat, who has never signed an autograph, has his own agent; Steve Pinkus of the William Morris Agency was the man who decided against a scheme to market Secretariat's waste products.

Not all of the ventures of the marketing people have been successful, no matter how well researched. Very few of them have approached the success—or the joy—that Bill Veeck had. But some have worked. And one is a textbook case in the creation, care and feeding of fans. The Atlanta Flames hockey franchise probably accomplished the greatest selling job in recent sports history.

Bringing hockey into the deep South was like bringing pork chops to a convention of orthodox rabbis; they had no background in it, no taste for it, no experience with it. Even the weather, which brought ice once an age, was against the success of hockey in the deep South. So it would be a selling job, a creating job, of the first order. Cliff Fletcher, the general manager of the Flames, said when the team started that "we never had any doubts." He must have been the only one.

Immediately after the team was created their publicist took some 15 members of the Atlanta press to the Stanley Cup play-offs so they could educate the fans back home. Both Atlanta newspapers were then persuaded to run detailed series on how the game was played.

The team's officials, including the debonair coach, Bernie Geoffrion, spoke at clubs around town, sometimes two and three times a day. Billboards were all over, shouting THE ICE AGE HAS COME TO ATLANTA. The same pitch was made on radio and television. A contest was held to select a name for the team, and 10,000 entries poured in. Fifty thousand copies of a booklet on the game, prepared by the NHL office, were given out. The team helped organize a fan club, which eventually drew 1000 members.

When it came time for the team, now called the Flames, to play the opening game, 14,568 people were there to watch. Final attendance figures were just under 13,000 per game for the first year. That was almost double what the Atlanta Hawks basketball team, which had a base and history to build on, achieved.

Who needs pantyhose?

FANNING THE FLAMES: YOU AND THE EYE
4

Mine eyes have seen the coming of another football year,
And there sits my old man with his cigarettes and beer.
His eyes are both in focus
On the color TV set,
And the games go on and on.

Players are runnin' left and right and he hollers what a game;
Even tho' I'm standing here, he can't recall my name.
He really is so worked up, he won't talk to me at all.
The game goes on and on
And it's drivin' me up the wall.
I always feared I'd lose my man
To another dame,
      But I never, ever dreamed
      It'd be a football game.*

The phrase is now part of the language: "football widow." She is the woman (usually referred to as "little") who stands dutifully by as her man plunks himself, his beer, his crackers and his program in front of the tube. She is blood sister to the baseball widow, basketball widow, hockey widow, *et al.* She is related by marriage to the armchair quarterback or manager. She is depicted as long-suffering but understanding. She under-

---

*"Another Football Year," © 1972 Wilderness Music Publishing Inc. Used by permission.

stands her husband. What she perhaps doesn't understand is that television has become the most important factor in fandom in this country.

There are people who have never been to a football game, who think it is insane to sit on an uncomfortable bench in freezing cold, needing binoculars to see anything, who are football fans. There are people who couldn't be bothered traveling to a ball park who are baseball fans. There are people who prefer to practice their putting in front of the TV console instead of on the green who are golf fans.

They don't have to go. More people see one year's World Series on television than have seen, in person, all the World Series in history. The 1973 Super Bowl was seen on television by 80 million people, the largest number of people ever to see a television program in the United States. The 1970 World Cup soccer playoffs, which were televised around the world, were seen by more people than any other event in history. Congress ruled against pro football blackouts and over one million prepaid seats weren't filled.

There are people who go to football games, baseball games, any game, *with* a television set. They sit down in their bleacher seats, prop their transistor jobs on their laps, plug in the earphones and watch the game. That way, they explain, they can *really* see what's going on.

There are fans—dedicated, knowledgeable fans—who go to games for the first time and are amazed that at the stadium there are no instant replays, no slow motion (usually referred to by the knowledgeable as "slow mo"). My God, not even any commercials. They may not have to be amazed much longer. The Landover, Maryland, arena of the Capital Bullets has huge television screens to show instant replay, and other stadiums and arenas are planning the same thing. At

FANNING THE FLAMES: YOU AND THE EYE 59

racetracks that have closed-circuit telecasts of the race, there are usually more people under the stands bunched by the set than there are out at the finish line.

There are rabid, enthusiastic, active fans who used to go to games and don't anymore. They'd just prefer not to freeze, not to fight the traffic, not to fight the crowds, not to pay the admission fee and the 60 cents for a frankfurter, 75 for a beer. Maybe in the past they enjoyed it, but now, well, they've just decided it's more comfortable, less strenuous, to sit in an uncrowded, warm home, with the best seat in the house. The beer is cheaper, too. So they sit at home and wait for their games to go on the air. And if they're not at home, they make sure to get there in time. Like Milton Berle and the "Texaco Shower of Stars" did before the invention of the isolated camera, televised sports has changed the social habits of a nation. During the 1974 Super Bowl, restaurants throughout the country were forced to close— no business. "Normally," said an official of Restaurant Associates, a major nationwide restaurant operator, "our places are filled at four P.M. on a Sunday. But on Super Sunday, there was a tremendous tailoff." Television rental agencies found that they were running short. Airline captains felt compelled to announce the scores. They really shouldn't have. There was an extraordinarily high number of canceled flight reservations during the hours of the game.

Variety, the bible of show business, has reported that motion-picture attandance on Monday nights "is in a real nosedive as a result of Monday night pro football." Some theaters, in fact, were considering shutting down on Monday nights during the football season. Restaurants could only entice people to eat out on Monday nights if they promised: "23-INCH COLOR TV!

60 GOD SAVE THE PLAYERS

Free Drinks During Half Time."; A self-styled gourmet restaurant in San Antonio, Texas, has installed individual color TV sets in one section of the restaurant so people can watch the game while eating. The Uptown Club, a restaurant in Birmingham, Alabama, urged possible patrons to "Watch the NFL Monday Night game with us . . . Your kind of folks—sports fans and girls. . . ."

If there is an important sports event on television, PTAs will cancel meetings, bowling leagues will postpone, working staffs will desperately try to finish their work in time to watch. And on Monday nights at Overlake Hospital in Seattle, according to one report, "There's an unwritten rule that no babies are to be born between 7:00 and 10:00 P.M., so that nothing interferes with the game." We all do our part.

Not only has television changed the habits of sports watchers, it has also changed the habits of sports itself. The World Series now starts on a Saturday, instead of the traditional Wednesday. There are now night games in the World Series. Football and hockey referees walk around with little beepers in their pockets so the TV people can tell them when to stop a game—and possibly a team's momentum—for a commercial. Along the benches of teams, in what used to be a sacrosanct area, the portable television camera patrols, pushing its lens into the faces of the sweating athletes. Coaches and referees and quarterbacks are wired for sound. Games begin at ten in the morning or five in the afternoon to accommodate "TV doubleheaders." Seats are blocked out at arenas, sometimes the best seats in the house, so that the TV cameras can have the angles they want. Soon, it is rumored, umpires will check the instant replays, rather than rely on their own impeccable judgment, to decide whether a man was safe or out. And if they don't, well, then the man by the set will continue to be a little more knowledgeable than the man on the baselines.

Perhaps the most dramatic illustration of the power of television on sports and on fans is how TV has literally created and saved entire leagues. The American Football League was a fledgling, a sickly infant trying to compete with the established National Football League, and failing. That is, until the American Broadcasting Company, lacking any major-league sports attractions of its own, decided to put the AFL on national TV. It was a two-edged sword: The league got both the prestige and a vastly increased audience. With the league on nationwide television, armchair fans were convinced it must be important, must be big-league. So the AFL did become big-league.

The same dynamics are in play with other newborn leagues. The American Basketball League died because it did not get a network-TV contract. It did not get the prestige and it did not get the wide following that only TV can give. The American Basketball Association is still hoping for a contract that will get it out of the tank towns and expand its following beyond a small coterie of fans. The organizers' hopes for the new World Football League rest almost entirely on television.

One of the major reasons, promoters believe, why soccer has never made it as a major sport in the United States is that it doesn't televise as well as most sports and therefore will never receive any large-scale television exposure.

It's not just the money—although money is a large part of it; a minute of commercial time at the last Super Bowl went for $210,000. If the networks make that much, the money filters down to the league. But a few years ago the National Hockey League was willing to sign a TV contract for very little money. In fact, they were glad to sign it. They knew that network exposure would give them the patina of class—and that almost unlimited viewing audience. The importance of television in creating fans is so critical that when a new league starts, in any sport, it immediately assigns franchises to New York and Los Angeles, the two largest TV markets in the country. The leagues rightly feel that the networks demand those two audiences if they are going to offer a contract.

But while it has created fans, teams, leagues and extra seats, television has also destroyed some things in sport. In the early Fifties boxing was thriving, with champions like Rocky Marciano and Sugar Ray Robinson. Then television stepped in with its "Friday Night Fights." The little fight clubs, the breeding grounds of the sport, could not compete. They went out of business, leaving boxing to the champions and top contenders in two or three classes. All or nothing. Thank you, Gillette. Perhaps the most prominent victim of television is minor-league baseball. Throughout the country, and particularly in the South and Midwest, minor-league baseball had always thrived, mainly because the teams needed only about 100,000 paid admissions a year to survive. But when television started to invade their markets, with "The Game of the Week," or the home games of the major-league team 300 miles away, minor-league attendance plummeted. Why go to some drafty minor-league park to see minor-league players when you could stay home and see Willie Mays on your set?

Ah, yes, the medium being the message, and all that. And no one seems to recognize that fact —and its companion, that television has become the most important factor in the creation of fans—no one more than the television people themselves.

Irv Brodsky, the head of public relations for

ABC Sports, is a smiling, friendly man, which is quite natural since he is part of a very profitable enterprise. With Roone Arledge as the prime mover, ABC Sports is one of the success stories in the industry. "There's no doubt about it," Brodsky says, "sports has made ABC. It's brought us parity with the other networks."

Still, Brodsky feels, TV has done more for sports than the other way around. "Yes, definitely, television can—and has—created sports fans. I think it does it in two major ways. Take 'Monday Night Football,' for instance. What that has done is to create a whole new kind of fan. These aren't fanatical fans, the kind of people who watch every football game they can possibly see. I mean, we get those too, but to get forty million people tuning in, you've got to get someone else. We've created fans who are interested in football as entertainment. Twenty-five percent of 'Monday Night Football' fans are women. That's as opposed to maybe ten percent on the weekends. One way you create fans is to take something they know and put new packaging on it. That's what we've done with 'Monday Night Football.' We've shown people a different way to see something."

That's one way. The other and most powerful method television employs to create fans is the most simple: exposure. Show people something they have not seen before, show them something they can't get to, or haven't heard of, or can't afford. "'Wide World of Sports,'" Brodsky proudly announces, "is the best example I know of in actually creating fans by just exposing them to something they hadn't seen before. When it went on the air in 1961, the American people didn't know, say, rugby from lacrosse. How many Americans then knew the names of skiers, or of gymnasts? Before '61, there were essentially three types of fans in this country: baseball fans and, to a lesser degree, football and basketball fans. So we put on 'Wide World' in '61 and a rabid baseball fan would turn it on, because, hell, there's nothing else on on Saturday afternoon. And then, goddamn, he sees that there is something else besides baseball.

"For the first time people knew the names of skiers. And that's what allowed Jean-Claude Killy to become a superstar. I mean, if not for 'Wide World,' do you think anybody in this country would have ever heard the name of Olga Korbut? But 'Wide World' made people interested in gymnastics and then made them interested in the Olympic gymnastics competition. And that made them interested in Olga Korbut.

"Exposure is the whole ball game in the world of sports. Take the American Football League. It wasn't very much when the network first picked it up. But it's a question of economics. Sports is a product. If you expose a product enough and the product is good—you can sell it."

Brodsky acknowledges that, yes, there are such things as television fans, people who do all their watching from in front of the tube. "There are fans who are TV fans, but I think that's a very small minority," Brodsky adds. "Usually what happens is that a guy sees something on TV and that whets his appetite for seeing the real thing. If TV does its job, it conveys the excitement of the event. And that should make the person want to get out and see the event in person. Because if TV did create 'studio' fans, it wouldn't be good for sports and it wouldn't, in the long run, be good for TV."

Brodsky is right when he says that television has created a whole new type of fan, one who is interested in sport as entertainment. But television has also created a whole new type of anti-

FANNING THE FLAMES: YOU AND THE EYE

fan, the football widow. Usually it's a figurative phrase. But not all the time.

During the summer of 1969, when the New York Mets were making history by making a run on the National League East pennant, they captured the imagination of the country. It was even said that New York City Mayor John Lindsay, a politician who had managed in his first term to antagonize almost all the diverse groups in a diverse city, was only able to win reelection by hitching his star to the Mets. (One of the people who said that was Mayor Lindsay.) People who didn't care about baseball, about sports, cared about the Mets. The involvement was visceral.

It was nowhere as intense as it was in the home of Mr. and Mrs. Frank Graddock, who lived in Ridgewood, Queens, not very far from Shea Stadium, the scene of all the excitement. Mr. Graddock was home from work this day, a warm one in June. A few miles away the Mets were meeting the Cubs in what was at the time the most important game of the season. Frank Graddock sat down comfortably in front of the set and was ready to watch the game when Margaret Graddock entered the room and said that it was time for her to watch "Dark Shadows," a soap opera about vampires, one of her favorite shows. Margaret Graddock wanted to find out if Quentin, who carries the curse of the werewolf, would be able to keep the mummy's hand he had pursued through the last few episodes. Frank Graddock said he was watching the game. Margaret turned the dial. Frank turned it back. In the ninth inning of the game, as the Mets and Cubs were fighting it out, Quentin was getting advice from Angelique, the witch, on how to shake the curse. Margaret Graddock tried to turn the dial again. Her husband punched her in the head and in the back. And again. Margaret went to bed to nurse her pains, and did not find out that Angelique had been bitten by a vampire. The game ended and Frank Graddock went into the bedroom to look at his wife, the police later reported.

Margaret Graddock, unlike Angelique, had been fatally injured. The next day Frank Graddock was charged with first-degree murder. Frank Graddock had become a sports widower.

Naturally, the term is not always that literal. But the phenomenon of sports widowhood is a growing one. When the games come on, the men assert their most chauvinistic tendencies. They do not wish to be disturbed. The women are shunted aside, told to occupy themselves with womanly pastimes, to come back after the games are over. Darrell Otto, an insurance man in Long Beach, California, built a $3000 den in his garage, complete with TV and bar, so he would not be disturbed by family or friends when his games were on. "I want to be able to enjoy those games with no interruptions," Mr. Otto explained.

But, perhaps influenced by women's liberation, women are not taking these affronts lying down. Schools have been formed in Los Angeles, Chicago and New York by women, for women, to teach them the intricacies of sports. The idea is, if you can't watch "Dark Shadows," then join 'em.

In Des Moines, Iowa, Mrs. Marilyn Sass started a class for football widows, "but the classes didn't go. I hope it will go next year." Among the game's intricacies that Mrs. Sass was going to teach was the appropriate attire for football viewing from the stands. "For instance, you don't wear a black satin dress and pearls to the Orange Bowl game," Mrs. Sass says.

"We are trying to solve a problem in communications," explains Pat Mason, the founder and director of New York's Now School. Patricia

Keane Mason is in her thirties, blonde, full-bodied, an emotional and outgoing artist "with a cosmic consciousness." Altogether, an interesting woman. She is married to a policeman, a football freak. "When there'd be a game on at night," Mrs. Mason remembers, "my husband would give me ten dollars to go out and eat. I didn't mind. At least I didn't have to cook."

But there have been times Patricia Mason *has* minded. There have been difficulties. "We have a good marriage, but when my husband would watch the game, he would ignore me. He didn't care if I was interested in the game or if I knew anything about it. And he didn't have any faith that I could learn."

The story of women in the Seventies is that they can never be told never. They have learned that anything they set their minds to they can accomplish. They are women, hear them roar. They have also learned that just because a man says something is so doesn't mean it is. "There was a time," Pat Mason remembers, "when my husband would turn the set on, I would turn it off, he would turn it on. Eventually he would win by being more stubborn because he was male. But finally I realized that didn't make him right."

Still, she was frustrated. She wanted to be part of this very important section of her husband's life. If all these silly games were important to him, then they were important to her. Finally, Mrs. Mason pleaded with Mr. Mason to teach her, to explain to her, to make manifest the intricacies of these games so that she too could become drugged. "Well, my husband *loved* teaching me. I guess he never tried before because he didn't think I would understand, but once he started——and I was able to grasp all of it——he was very proud of me. In fact, I think most husbands would be proud of their wives if they learned the games. I think they understand that it means the wife really cares about her husband."

There are, Pat Mason admits, some men who would not exactly feel that way. "Let's face it," she says, "being a sports fan is probably the last bastion of male chauvinism. And men want to keep it that way. That's why they go to such lengths to watch their games. That's why on their Sundays they try so hard to avoid the women."

Chauvinism? The men deny it. Pat Mason's husband, Al, a police sergeant, said he liked to hide away in front of the tube because . . . just because. He enjoyed it. He wasn't trying to drive his wife away. He wasn't putting a wall between them. Chauvinism? No, he explained. It was just that he had his interests and she had hers.

Mrs. Mason takes a more politico-sexual view of the matter. "It's all based on a social structure of classifications," she says. "Men are one class and women are another. According to this whole structure, men are supposed to have time by themselves, to do what they want. To 'go out with the guys' if they want that. But women, you see, aren't supposed to have any time for themselves, to have any interests which aren't the family interests."

Dr. Henry Kellerman, a psychologist and psychoanalyst in New York City, takes a different politico-sexual view. "Women are forcing themselves to become interested in sports only so they can be with their men and so the men will be more interested in them," he says. "That's certainly not a result of liberation. It's just further subordinating themselves to gain access to their men."

Mrs. Mason is a little more understanding. "The funny thing is, men generally feel guilty about watching their games. And that just makes it worse. They know they've been wrong, so when the women confront them with it they either ignore them or become hostile.

"There's also a sexual aspect to it. I think sometimes when men get bored sexually with their wives, these games become their sexual outlet. I remember when I was on David Susskind's television show discussing football. He told me he liked football more than he liked sex."

Evenhandedly, Mrs. Mason also blames women for allowing the whole thing to happen. "If a man does go into his den, closes the door and watches his games all day and night, it's partially the woman's choice, too. A lot of women don't want to be involved in their husband's lives. They really aren't that interested. But I think all of that is changing."

Linda Singer, a young Long Island housewife, is hip and forward-looking. Still, on a television show devoted to football widowhood she said, "They're entitled to their thing. Except why does their thing have to take sixteen hours a day?"

But things are changing. When Pat Mason started her Now School, the response was immediate and large. "We even got one man who signed up. He wanted to go to the classes with his wife. He said he was a football widower."

The women started learning and soon were able to sit in front of the set and talk to their men about crackbacks, seamless zones and end-arounds. "As women learn their men's games, as they become just as much fans as their husbands, I think women are going to find sports to be a beautiful expansion of consciousness," envisions Patricia Mason, wide-eyed. "I don't know how, exactly, but I think it will be."

The family that roots together stays together. At home. In front of the tube. Endlessly.

ALEX AND BILL
5

Yankee Stadium, the one that was, wasn't all monuments and grandeur. It is dreary there this day, the September sky hanging low, just over the ornate facade. The feeling is gray all over: the New York Yankees, 15 games out of first place, playing the Cleveland Indians, 22 games out of first place. The grayest place of all is deep in the mezzanine section, directly behind home plate. The roof of the upper deck hangs so low here that no outside light, however dim, is let in. The aisles and the corridors here are hospital-colored and grimy. The snack stands behind in the runway are closed and boarded up, because there are less than 5000 people here this day. But Alex and Bill are here.

They are almost always here, deep in the mezzanine, their scorebooks and statistics sheets spread out in front of them. They'll usually have a radio, or two, earplugs in their ears, to listen to another game, somewhere. The seats around them will be empty, folded up. They like to sit in an empty area where no one will bother them, where they can spread out. Alex and Bill, who are here during good days and bad, know where those areas are. And the regulars, the ushers, the Yankee front-office people, the concessionaires, they know Alex and Bill. Of course, they don't really *know* them. They don't know their last names, or if they have last names. They know them just as Alex and Bill. They don't know what they do, or if they do anything, anything other than coming to the baseball games. They know that the two don't bother anybody, and so no one bothers them. They know that Alex and Bill are just two plain people in a dreary place on a dreary day.

Alex Zavras and Bill Stimers fit the mood of the day. Alex, the older one, is wearing a faded gray suit with the jacket's sleeves too long. He is balding, with only a fringe of hair left. His eyes are deep-set, gray and somewhat milky. His face is sallow, seemingly featureless, slack-jawed. He is 56, but he could be any age. His manner is laconic.

Bill is younger, 26, more outgoing, brighter-faced. He has a mop of curly blond hair sitting on a square, badly complexioned face, which sits on top of a blocky body. He is wearing a light-green cardigan. His pants are light green, too.

Alex has been going to see Yankee baseball games for 33 years. He went to his first baseball game in September 1941. It was a Sunday, he remembers, a doubleheader against the Boston Red Sox. "Red Ruffing was pitching the first game." For 23 of the 33 years, in addition to going to Yankee Stadium, Alex would also go on the road with the Yankees. "I really can't afford that anymore though, now. This is the only place I go. I don't go no place else."

Bill has been going to Yankee games for 22 years. "My father is a baseball fan and he brought me to Oldtimers' Day in 1952. That was the first time ever. I've been coming ever since."

Alex and Bill, then, are not nouveau fans, fans who go to the games to be seen as much as to see. They don't believe the game is a prelude to a couple of martinis and a discussion. They are not fashionable fans, nor flashy ones. Nor are they intelligent, clever or attractive. Their lives, to others, must seem unbearably dreary. Psychologists might say they are the perfect examples of dull people who must get their excitement vicariously. All Alex and Bill know is that they're nobody special, doing nothing special. "I don't see why you'd want to talk to us," Bill says. "We're just fans."

They are "just fans" the way Richard Nixon is just another Whittier College grad. Alex says he doesn't go anywhere else but the baseball games. He says, "Baseball is the most important thing in my life." Bill, perhaps because he's younger and not quite so settled, admits that he also enjoys football and hockey. "I got tickets to their games, too." Sports are monumentally important to him, but his family, he says, is more important. "I care about baseball, I care about the Yankees, but I also care about my family and I care about my job."

Bill is a machine operator in a bakery and lives in Brentwood, Long Island, with his parents. "Living with my parents," Bill explains, "I don't have to pay any rent. They support me." That's how, even though his salary isn't much, he's able to be at all the games, except those played while he's working, every year. "Well, my father sometimes helps me out. He lends me money during the summer, and then I pay him back during the winter."

Alex, who is a stockroom boy in a paper company, lives alone in Manhattan. His financial situation is a little more tenuous, which is why he had to give up going on the road. "I used to live with my parents, too," he says. "Then they died. When I was living with them, you'd just pay for your food, so you could go on the road trips. Now I'm all alone and I gotta pay forty-six dollars a week rent and I can't do it. It's tough." Alex manages to go to the games through careful management. "It's not easy," he says, "but in the winter I save. I put three dollars away every week. It helps me get through the summer."

They also get through with a little help from their friends. "We know a lot of people at the stadium," Bill says, "and a lot of times, particularly if it's not too crowded, they'll let us in for nothing."

The transistor radio was suddenly turned on louder, and the sounds of another game could be heard. Bill quickly turned toward it, not missing a word, wanting to know, to know *exactly*, how the Mets were doing. Both Alex and Bill are Met fans, too. But it is the Yankees, the erstwhile Bronx Bombers, who hold that special spot in their hearts.

The team is no longer the one they grew up with. The Yankees aren't in the Bronx and aren't bombers anymore and don't draw the crowds, the coverage, the excitement. Still, if you grew up with them, they are still the Yankees, even on the dreariest of days. That is why Alex and Bill are here.

"I've been close to the team all these years," says Bill, the younger one. "All these years they gave us a lot of excitement. So much excitement. We got their glory. I was lucky to see Mickey Mantle all these years. I've been so lucky."

Alex digs into his back pocket for his wallet, a dog-eared, brown folder. "Look at this," he says. There is a picture of Alex, perhaps ten years younger but looking much the same, with Ralph Houk, the former Yankee manager. It is a graying picture, seamed with deep cracks. Houk is wearing his "let me take a picture of you" smile. Alex looks nervous. "And look at this one, too." This is a picture, also graying and cracked, of Alex and Mel Allen, the former Yankee broadcaster. Alex is perhaps 15 years younger in this one, and here he is smiling a little. "These people are just such nice people," he is saying. "Look how they care."

74 GOD SAVE THE PLAYERS

It is very difficult for Alex to explore why he cares so much; why baseball, why the Yankees, have been his life since 1941. He is not used to anyone being concerned with what is inside his head, so he is not able to answer quickly. He waits for the reason to turn up in his head. "It's just what I like to do," he says finally. Then he tries to explain by talking about others, about the people he knows, the ones who don't like baseball, who don't like the Yankees. "I don't understand it," he says. "I don't understand why they don't care. They don't ask me anymore about my caring, though. They know how I feel. And anyway, I don't have that many friends who don't like the Yankees. All the people I like like the Yankees."

Sometimes, Bill says, the people at his bakery might poke a little fun at him about all the baseball games. "Since the team hasn't been as good, they make fun of the Yankees sometimes. They say, 'How can you listen to a team like that? They're no good.' But I don't let it bother me. And if the Yankees are playing a day game and I'm at work, when it's two o'clock I still take my break and I turn the game right on. It doesn't bother me if they make fun. And anyway, most of my friends I met at baseball games."

That is how Alex and Bill met, how they formed their partnership and came to be considered an entry, the Rosencrantz and Guildenstern of the American League. "It was in 1970," Bill remembers. "I guess we had each seen each other around the stadium. When you get to the stadium before the gates even open, there's not too many people here. And the two of us were always here. So we just started talking, talking about the Yankees, and about baseball. We'd talk about records, about the different players we met, and we just sort of decided to stick together.

ALEX AND BILL 75

We've been together ever since."

"Ever since" means all the Yankee night games, all games on Saturdays and Sundays, all games on holidays. "It's hard to get to many of the day games, with having to work and all," Alex explains. The two have made excursions together away from the stadium, but for baseball reasons. "We go down to the hotels a lot to see the players," Bill says. "It's easy to find out where they're staying. Most of the teams stay at the same places anyway. We go down there because it's exciting to talk to the players. Oh, we talk to them about records and things like that. They're always nice. They always give you their autographs."

Alex doesn't collect autographs. He points to his head. "I got all the autographs up here," he says. "I don't need them."

Bill is still talking about going down to the hotels. "They're always nice," he says again. Always? Every time? Bill doesn't seem to want to admit that there has ever been a ballplayer who wasn't nice. "Well," he finally says, "Mickey Lolich, he wasn't very nice. We went up to talk to him and he wasn't nice at all. He was a little mad. All he kept saying was, 'No autographs . . . no autographs.' "

Bill takes all his autographs and puts them away in his basement, where he puts all his baseball mementos. "I got a big bookcase in my basement and I got all the yearbooks, all the teams, every year for about the last twenty years. I have a picture, an autographed picture, of Don Larsen down there, too."

Alex, although he doesn't collect autographs, does collect his own kind of baseball memorabilia. "I have the records of every American League pitcher, his won-lost record, earned-run average, everything, of every American League pitcher since 1946. I kept them all myself. I also got all the baseball guides since 1942."

"I've got all the football and hockey guides, too," Bill adds.

Alex and Bill keep looking away, watching very closely what is happening on the field. They don't cheer, jump up, scream, berate, plead. But they sit hunched forward, expectantly. When they do move they seem to do it in unison.

The game is over. The Yankees, once again, have lost. The few thousand people in the stands shuffle passionlessly to the exits. No one runs onto the field, no bases are stolen, no sod is kicked up. The ushers have all left. The press box is empty, the reporters running downstairs to get their stories and then get out.

Alex and Bill do not seem upset that their team has lost. If anything, they seem resigned. It doesn't really matter that much—although they would deny it—whether their team has won or lost. For them, it's like deciding whether your wife is pretty or homely. Either way, she's still your wife.

Yankee Stadium is homely, but it is Alex's and Bill's home. This is where they are comfortable, where their identities reside. Alex and Bill don't seem to have much else in the world, but that is someone else's perspective, not theirs. To them, life is okay. They have everything they want, everything they need and everything they can handle. Sports, baseball, the New York Yankees baseball team fills them.

Alex and Bill are gathering their things, their radios still on. They head down to the press box, to ask a Yankee front-office man if he has any extra guides he could give them. There is one more question for them: Is there anything you don't like about baseball? Anything?

"No," Bill says.

THE VOICE OF THE PEOPLE
6

The assistant public-relations man of the New York Mets picked up the phone and said, "Yes, can I help you?" The voice on the other end was adolescent, nervous, vaguely embarrassed. He was a great fan, he said, the number-one fan; he just loved the team, went to as many games as he could. He liked just about all the players, had gotten autographs of some of them, wanted to get more, wanted to write to some of his favorite players.

"How, uh, could I, uh, write to some of your players?" he wanted to know.

The Mets, like almost all professional teams, have entire departments that handle the huge amounts of incoming fan mail, the requests for stickers, for autographs, for pictures, for inside information, for tips on how to play the game. They get lots of phone calls, too. The PR man patiently answered the question. "It's very simple," he said. "Just send the letter to your favorite player, care of the New York Mets, Shea Stadium, Queens, New York. And it'll get right to him."

And, of course, a week or so later, a letter came to the PR man addressed, "Favorite Player, New York Mets, Shea Stadium, Queens, New York."

The letters come to the teams, to the individuals, from all over the country, from all different types. Mostly, it's the kids. They want to tell the players not to worry, that *they* believe, that there's somebody out there who cares. They want, very much, to make sure that the players know there's someone who cares. They want affirmation that their faith is not misplaced. Tangible affirmation.

Dear Mr. Murcer,
I like the way you macke flying leeps for the ball. I think you bat great. I hope you ceep mackeing Home Run's. I think you will get to go in the playoffs. and if you can come to my house to eat lunch lefrak city copenhagen 3-J and what do you want to eat if you can. come at 1:30 july 23 try to answer this letter

Sincerely,
Bobby

Dear Team,
I am a great fan of yours. I try to watch all of your games, but sometimes my parents say I should go out and get some fresh air. Please send me your autograph. Here is my autograph.

Gregg

Dear Sir,
I would like to have two sets of the Hawks, if you could. Thank you.

Andy B.

Dear Mr. Aaron,
Mr. Aaron, I would like to know if you could send me a Autograph Picture. My old picture was ripe by my sister, and a little help from my cat, George.

From a Big Fan,
Ross C.

Dear Larry Dierker,
My NAME is matt I AM a catcher for the little league. could you send me two auto-

THE VOICE OF THE PEOPLE

graphed pictures of you in action. Be in the dugout on june third I will be be there. Look for me. If I see you I will yell Larry. I'll be there.

Matt

Dear Timothy J. Rossovich,

I love you. You're so darn crazy. The things you do turn me sometimes on so far that I have a hard time returning back to normal reality. Show me how to be as crazy as you. I need your inspiration to guide me through my gridiron days. If you're ever around the area, stop by at 2212 East 33rd Street, right off route 57.

Yours craziest,
Mike T.

P.S.: Write down address before you eat the paper.

Dear Mr. Csonka,

My little brother had an autograph pitcher of you that I lost. He's been crying for a week about it. I know how these pictures are very valuable, but I was wondering if you could send him another one with your autograph again. I hope so, because my brother really hates me now, Sincerely,

Tommy

Dear Sir,

Since I live here in Seattle there are no major league games to go to so could you send me these two autographs on the card with the players name on it. Dave May and George Scott. If not, could you do a good job forging. Thank you and good luck.

A brewer fan
Rick S.

In exchange for affirmation, they will give affirmation. So you're hitting .219, lead the league in hitting into triple plays and afflictions of the lower intestine? You say your manager doesn't like you and the ballboy snickers when you go up to the plate? You're thinking of committing suicide if you're put on the suicide squad? It's all right, it's okay. Just read the mail the clubhouse man left in your cubicle.

Dear Graig Nettles
You are the best third basement. Even better than brooks Robinson. You are second in home runs.
How come you wanted to be a third basement?

Sincerely,
Tommy E.

Dear George Medich
I am your fan. I think you are a Great pitcher. My Birthday is coming up. Can I have an autograph of you. I am your idol.

Your fan,
Mike L.

Dear Mr. Murcer
I hope that the yankees come in first place this year. I am sure that you will hit more than 60 home runs this year. I am sorry that the Yankees did not win last year, but they will surely win this year. In your next game will you please hit a home run for me?

your fan,
Robert Q.

Dear Johnny Unitas,
I love your team and I want a picture of you and your team. I want one of Lou, John Mackey, and Tom Matte and the center. I

THE VOICE OF THE PEOPLE

forgot his name. Billy Ray, I want a picture of him and one of Jerry Hill, Earl and Bobby Curtus to and your coach Don. If you can't get all of these pictures then let Don get them.

> Thank you,
> Ray

It's not always the kids who write. The older kids write, too. These are the people who might see an athlete in a restaurant, whisper, "Do you know who *that* is?" but don't have the courage to go up and say something directly. They might sit in the stands, screaming, "You bum! You miserable cur!" but when the object of their affections turns to see who is doing the imprecating, they become very quiet. Still, there is something about writing a letter, sending a piece of fan mail, that enables these people to express themselves, their desires, their ideas. Perhaps for that one moment, that fraction of time when the player reads the letter, he is theirs. The writer owns him, his attention. He can tell him what he does right, does wrong, why. And he can tell the player something about himself. For those few seconds, without any back talk, he owns him.

Horace,
Congratulations to you Horace. By opening up a 2 run inning by beating out a single to short and no question helping your team and mine against the Brewers 11 to 4. It is men like you and few others who make base ball one of the best sports to day. Keep it up Horace & may God bless all.

> Sincerely,
> Frank

If you have a photo in your proud club Yankee uniform would you send 1 to a 75

82 GOD SAVE THE PLAYERS

year old broken down and benched sports fan for my den room. Many thanks Horace.

Dear Mr. _____

My name is Michael _____ and I am an ex drug addict. Since I been off drugs everything in my life been going downhill, but before I really say what I want to say, I want you to know it's very hard for me to write on paper the things I want to say, but here it goes. I need an opportunity to talk to the ballplayers, because for the last three months they were the only thing that was keeping me going, and now even that wish is going down the drain. I am getting so depressed now because I can't take another thing that I wanted to happen so much fail. So I am begging you sir to give me a chance to let the ballplayers know how important it is to me that they win their division. If you decide against my request please destroy the letter, but if you decide in favor of my request I would be so grateful.
Thank you.

Dear Brother in Christ:

I want to thank you for your letter in regard to the football for the purpose of using in my message. This will make you feel as good as it did me, I know.

When I received your letter I read it and read it and I started asking how in the world a poor Baptist preacher with 4 children and a wife was going to get $25 to spend on a football just to use for an illustration. This past Wednesday night I was out by myself and I prayed this prayer, "Lord, I feel that this football would help young people to get a lot more from this "football sermon." If you want me to use it You will have to send the $25.

The next morning I was out in our little town and a dear old gentleman hollered at me and said "get in the car, preacher." I got in. He said, "I have a little something that I want to give you. Don't mention that I gave it to you. I just felt led to give it and I know that you can use it." I thanked him. I thanked him because I knew that the Lord was answering my prayer.

So enclosed you will find the $25 for the football to be used for the Glory of God and I thank the Good Lord for leading this precious old saint of His to give this preacher two tens and a five. Praise the Lord.

I may be just a bit selfish, but I'm asking the Lord to help the Cowboys be the World Champions this season. God bless you in your work is my prayer.

Frequently, the older fans will send in letters telling their teams and players how to play the game, what they are doing wrong and what they have uncovered through months of careful observation. The New York Giants football team once received a letter from a "great fan" who offered some advice about how to stop Jim Brown. Brown, the great Cleveland fullback, was the Giants' next opponent and the most dangerous player in the league. The fan wrote that he had spent three years studying Brown's moves and discovered that he always went in the direction opposite to his hand stance. Very interesting. Might be worth checking out.

The Giants checked it out. "We checked it back on our files and saw it was true," Don Smith, a former Giants official, remembered. "So we prepared for it and figured, Oh boy, we're gonna really fall on him. We couldn't wait for the game to start."

The game started, and on the very first play from scrimmage Jim Brown put his left hand down and the entire Giant defense expectantly slanted to the right. And—you guessed it—Brown raced left. "For fifty yards," Smith recalled.

Then there are the letters that cannot be broadly classified. They each fall into a classification of their own.

> Dear Sir,
> Just because I'm a poor kid doesn't mean I can't like the Yankees. Well my mom only make a dollar every three days. My father doesn't work because he is dead. But I do have a hope that will help us. Well my buddy said he'd pay me a dollar for every decal from the Yankees and a quarter for every sticker of the Yankees. So please help!
> thank you
> Stevie

> Dear Mr. Williams,
> I am 10 years old and a great fan of yours. I would like to ask for the old bases of the team. I would like it if you would give them to me.
> Thank you.
> Andrea

> Dear Colts,
> Would you please send me an autographed picture of you. I am not sure but I think I saw you play once. If I didn't I will.
> Your friend,
> Rudy

THE VOICE OF THE PEOPLE 85

Dear God,
Thank you for my bike and my turn-around and my trick-or-treat candy. And thank you for me, and all life, and for the mountain, and for Saturday, and for leaves, and for food and for the Monday Night Football game.

Dolph

Dear Mr. Wolff:
I want to commend you for the excellent manner in which you broadcast the Senators' baseball games. You have the faculty of effectively describing the various plays during the games which enables the listener to clearly understand what is going on in the field of play.

I have heard a number of favorable comments concerning the outstanding manner in which you broadcast the games.

Sincerely,
J. Edgar Hoover.

At one time Ben Davidson, a massive brutishly handsome man, was a star in the National Football League. He twirled his elegant mustache, sacked flashy quarterbacks and achieved renown. He even got a part in a brutishly handsome porno flick, *Behind the Green Door*. Then, as quickly as it had come, it was gone. Davidson languished on the bench, a member of the taxi squad. His opinions were not sought, he was not offered commercials, he was not offered roles in any kind of movies. There was also another indication of the public decline of Ben Davidson: "In the old days, I got five fan letters a day. Now I'm lucky if I get two in a week. Doesn't anybody want to write to me anymore?"

CHRIS, AND HENRY, TOO
7

Chris Drago, originally from Mobile, Alabama, now of Memphis, Tennessee, is white, 32 years old, unmarried, self-supporting. He is a graduate of Southwestern State University, also of Memphis, with a degree in economics. He has taught economics at Lemoyne-Owen College and at Lane College. He has worked for the Federal Health, Education and Welfare Department, assigned to the University of Tennessee where he was a demographer. He is bushily bearded, southern-accented, friendly. And at the age of 32, Chris Drago has given up teaching economics, has given up working for HEW and has decided to follow Henry Aaron around.

Henry Aaron, of Atlanta, black, 40 years old, also originally from Mobile, Alabama, is a baseball player, one of the greatest of his or any generation. With 713 home runs going into the 1974 baseball season, he was one home run short of Babe Ruth's all-time record. Until he hit home run number 714 to tie Babe Ruth, until he hit home run number 715 to pass Babe Ruth, Chris Drago planned to be with him. He would be with him if Henry Aaron was in Atlanta (272 miles from Memphis) or San Francisco (1768 miles from Memphis) or Montreal (1163 miles from Memphis). He would be with him until that day, and for many days beyond. It was just something that Chris Drago felt he must do. It was also better than teaching economics.

Drago is intelligent, verbal and communicative. He is also a man of singular opinions and actions. He was one of the very few white men who joined

James Meredith on his trans-Mississippi walk in 1966. He can discuss consumer actions—he is involved in the Tennessee Consumer Alliance—as well as black-white relations. He enjoys talking about music; he is a musician and was once a record producer. He enjoys talking about buying land in the Ozark Mountains and has written a book about it. But when the questions revolve around his devotion to Henry Aaron, his decision to follow him around, his compulsion with almost all sports, he finds it difficult to communicate. He tends to look off into the distance, rub his beard, walk around the room. Time passes. Finally, pressed for an answer, he shrugs his shoulders. His eyes widen. "I suppose it's true that I am more involved than the average man or the average fan. I guess . . . I don't know whether I can pinpoint exactly why. But it's real important to me. Real important."

Right now, the most important thing in the life of Chris Drago, more important than the Memphis Tams basketball team, more important than the Alabama University football team, more important than anything else, is Henry Aaron and his quest for a baseball statistic. Drago is able and willing to trace exactly how Henry Aaron's quest became so important to him.

"I was just a young boy in Mobile and I was a big Braves fan, when they were in Boston. I don't know why, but I was a Boston Braves fan for some reason. I remember reading about Hank when he was playing for Jacksonville, the Braves farm team. I was reading about him all the time because he was a local boy, too. I remember he was leading the league in everything except hotel accommodations. He was doing so good I knew he was going to be playing for the Braves someday, and I thought it was great. Here was a guy from Mobile playing for my favorite team. So

I followed his career from the beginning and I followed it very carefully."

Drago, because he is perceptive and has been around, understands there are a lot of people who check the papers, check the tube, hit a few games to follow the progress of an athlete, without becoming as emotionally involved. Most people don't get any more attached than the fine-tuning dial. "I guess it was just different with me," he explains.

"After about ten years, Hank was becoming a real good power hitter and I started calculating ahead, and I started talking that he was going to end up high on the all-time homer list. In the early or maybe mid-Sixties, I started telling guys, mostly this one guy, Kelly Thomas—now there's a guy you could write about, until he got married; now that guy doesn't go *anywhere*—I started telling him that Hank might do it, that he had a real chance. When I realized several years ago that Hank was actually going to do it, I started calculating again and, well, at first I didn't plan to follow him around all the time. That was because I really didn't think there was any chance of my doing anything like that. So then I just planned on seeing the event. I just planned on seeing number 714 and number 715. I was going to be satisfied with that. I was going to go see the event, no matter where it was."

There are many events, many sights that seem to cry out for first-person witness. I, for instance, would like to see the ancient Japanese tea ceremony. I would like to see the Taj Mahal. Seeing a baseball record being surpassed is somewhere down the list.

Not for Chris Drago. "Why? Why do I want to see the event so much? Well, number one, I followed a man's career for twenty years, and it'd be pretty foolish not to see him tie and break a record. A historic record. I remember when I was a young kid, they said nobody'd ever break it. It's quite an achievement, you know. I mean, if it was Willie Mays, or somebody else, I'd still be interested in the event. I'd want to see it, too. But with Hank, well, I just gotta see it. I just can't miss it."

Drago, in fact, admits that he doesn't just want to *be* there, he wants to be at a specific somewhere when he is there. " I don't want to be just in the stands, I want to be at a certain point. I want to be in the front row of the left-field bleachers on the aisle. There are only three seats that I find acceptable in Atlanta Stadium, and I have to be in one of those particular seats."

Then the idea metamorphosed. It was no longer sufficient for Drago to be there only for the event. He wasn't just going to show up, full-blown like a child of Zeus, only on the day or night the event occurred.

"Originally, oh maybe two years ago when I was making my first definite calculations and thought that Hank would be doing it in the summer of '74, I figured I just would take a leave of absence. But with my job being phased out, it worked out perfectly.

"It was really just a matter of circumstances," Drago explains. "I was working as a demographer, mostly doing planning and evaluation in the health field, at the University of Tennessee, on a grant from HEW. Then in December of '72 we were notified that Nixon had not put us into his budget. Then in January I was notified that my particular job was being phased out the next June. That was when I made my plans to be in Atlanta."

The job officially ended on June 29, 1973. On June 30, 1973, Chris Drago was in Atlanta, Georgia—specifically, Atlanta Stadium, the left-field bleachers, front row, aisle seat. He had driven down from Memphis to Atlanta in a 1959 white Buick he had bought for eight dollars. It had been abandoned, didn't run, but throughout the remainder of the 1973 season Drago put 12,000 miles on it by going back and forth to Atlanta. With him in the car he took books and papers dealing with projects he was involved in. "People think I haven't been doing anything at all, but I took all that stuff each time with me and I did more work than a lot of people do normally." He also took with him a baseball glove, very well broken in, that cost 37 cents at Goodwill Industries and which he wears at the games. He took his butterfly net to catch any balls that might come near. He also took with him his banner. The banner, which he always hangs down the front of the left-field bleachers, has a large, multicolored bull's-eye, and to the right of it a number. Going into the 1974 season the number was 714. "The idea is the number is always one more than Hank has," Drago explains. "The number is what he's aiming at. You see, the 'seven' is stationary. But we have a 'fifteen' ready when Hank gets 714. The 'fourteen' is just attached with some sticky kind of stuff. You can pull it right off."

With his glove, his net and his bull's-eye, his papers and his Buick, and with $50 in his pocket, Drago drives to Atlanta. Many times, he would stay at a Scottish Inn near the Atlanta Stadium for six dollars a night. Other times, driving down with his roommate, in his roommate's van, they would find a closed gas station, pull the van in and sleep in the back of it. For a shower, they would run over to the local "Y." For food, Drago would make sure to eat very carefully, looking for the all-you-can-eat places. Or perhaps he would get in touch with some of the people he knows in Atlanta. All in all, it has been a life lived tenuously, on the brink of insolvency.

Money is not important to him. "I just want

enough money to get around and drink my beer," he says. He is not acquisitive. He can live, if he must, stripped down to the essentials. Sports is one of the essentials. Money is not important, but to support his habit he is careful with it. "Since I left my job, I've kept a record of every penny I've spent. I've found out how little I need to live. The reason I write everything down is that I know if I have to write it down, then I won't spend it. And I know I can't spend it. It's not easy living for a year and a half without a job."

Drago wants it made clear, though, that he is not a Salvation Army case, at least not yet. "I'm not a pauper," he says. "I could afford to live. But I had to be careful, very careful. I didn't know how long I was going to go without a job. What I was trying to do was to live for twelve months on eight months' salary. That's because after I was phased out I had two months of annual leave stored up. So that gave me eight months' salary. I just tried to spread it around.

"So far, it's worked out fine. But if the money runs out, then I'll just have to start taking some pickup work. Work for Manpower. Do anything. In October '74, after it's all over, I'll start looking for what I might call a real job."

When he is not in Atlanta, or in Tuscaloosa, Alabama, watching Alabama football games, or going to the Sugar Bowl in New Orleans, or watching the Cardinals play in Saint Louis, Drago spends his time in a low-rent, comfortable, somewhat ramshackle clapboard house he shares with one and a half roommates. The half is a friend from Texas who spends half his time in Texas. Drago's bedroom has the look of disaster about it. All around, on the floor, are boxes filled with files, statistics, memorabilia. "They're not very organized files, but I do keep massive files. That's part of the fun for me." On his desk next to the bed there are envelopes scattered all around, and scattered all around the envelopes are ticket stubs——baseball, college football, pro football, college basketball, pro basketball——ticket stubs all over. "My collection," Drago says proudly.

Chris Drago is not concerned with outward impressions, or, for that matter, with outsiders' impressions. When he was involved in the poor-people's campaign in Memphis, when it was not such a liberated South as it is today, he learned about marching to his own drummer. His house is comfortable, convenient, very much lived in. His roommate has a magnificent beer-can collection in the dining room. The stero is well equipped. The neighbor's cat makes house calls to get rid of the mice. Drago is the same casual, comfortable way about himself. His dress is nondescript. His pants are probably chinos, his shoes probably Hush Puppies. His glasses are somewhat heavy, bulky tortoise-shell frames, unfashionable but effective. He likes his beer.

Drago doesn't believe he's undergoing any hardships, financial or otherwise, in his quest of Aaron's quest. Anyway, to him that is beside the point. He feels that if someone wants to do something, what difference does it make how difficult it is——or appears to be——to do it? What difference does it make how much it costs? If that's what he wants to do, hell, then he does it. What difference does it make what other people think?

Like most dedicated, involved fans, Chris Drago is friends mostly with others who are dedicated, involved fans. It's not that those are the only people he meets; it's that those are the kind of people to whom he gravitates. His roommate, Harvey Caughey, has taken many of the trips to Atlanta with him. Caughey also intends to be there for the big home runs. "But, you see, to Caughey," says Drago, "he's just going for the event. He just knows it's important. I guess if Hank does it in some place like San Francisco, Caughey won't be there. But if he could see it, he'd be there if Mays was doing it or anybody. To me, I *have* to be there. It's Hank that's going to be doing it."

In a nation where the color of your skin frequently denotes the way you color your world, Chris Drago is an anomaly. Being a fan in this nation usually means being strung out along racial and ethnic lines. Ask most Italians who the greatest ballplayer ever was and the answer is Joe DiMaggio. Black people grew up on Jack Johnson, Joe Louis and then Jackie Robinson and now Muhammad Ali. Joe Louis, the "brown bomber," was a "credit to his race." Maurice Richard, the hockey player, admitted that he represented the aspirations of all French-Canadians. Every fighter with an Irish name was always called "Irish" Joe McGuffy, or "Irish" Bobby Cassidy by the publicity people. The New York Rangers hockey team once had a goaltender named Lorne Chabot. Because of the large Jewish population of New York City, they changed his name to Chabotsky to give the fans someone to identify with. The Jewish fans still didn't come; they still couldn't believe that a Jewish boy would be a hockey player. Eventually, the Rangers changed Chabot's name back. The Atlanta Hawks basketball team, predominantly black, almost mortgaged the franchise so they could sign Pete Maravich, white, and give the white fans a role model.

A fan generally chooses his heroes because he has something in common with them, because he can identify with them, because in some sense they represent him. Chris Drago, white, has chosen Hank Aaron, black.

"Yessir," he says, "Hank Aaron is my hero.

That's the word. The black-white thing? I'll tell you, I never even think about it. It is just not a significant factor for me. I'm interested in a man who's a great baseball player and I just love to watch him perform."

There aren't many in this country as color-blind as Chris Drago. Surely, in Memphis, Tennessee, in the South, somewhere, there has been some adverse reaction to this white man following around this black man. "I haven't, honestly, detected even one case of it. You know, they had some stories about me in the local papers and rather than the black-white thing what completely overwhelmed them, I think, is the idea that I could arrange to live for an extended period of time the way I have. That's a dream to a lot of people. The whole racial factor was buried under that."

But the reaction of his friends to the way he has arranged his life has been mild, he says. "The people that really know me are not that surprised, I think. They know I'm going to do some unusual things and this is just one of them. People who don't know me, I guess they look at me as kinda strange.

"But, you know, I think most people think what I'm doing is really great because they'd like to be able to say the hell with it and do something they really want to do. But they can't because they got a house, or a family, or something. Maybe they don't wanta go watch baseball, but they got something in the back of their heads that they want to do. I guess the word is 'jealousy.' "

In a society of Horatio Alger, the Judaeo-Christian ethic and the achievement drive, the underachiever is the freak. There is jealousy—and perhaps resentment—because the freak has shown that the mold can be broken, that we don't have to stay trapped in little cubbyholes.

"Well, there hasn't been much of that kind of resentment," Drago says. "At least not that much that I've heard right out in front. Well, I did hear this librarian when I was down there getting some books. She was talking about my roommate, but she really meant me, too. She was talking about the idea of a guy with a college education not producing the maximum——you know, not saving the world. I didn't say anything but I was perfectly prepared to defend myself. I mean, it was totally absurd. I feel like I did plenty with my teaching and in the regional medical program. I was just gonna tell her if I had a record for the past eight years of not doing anything I'd feel bad. But I don't because this is something I want to do. I've made a lot of damn sacrifices. When I was teaching, I made thirty-five hundred a year. I could barely pay my rent. Hell, I'm not ashamed."

He has no guilt about being driven to do the things he does, because he is not driven, he says. He is not compulsive. He doesn't have to go lie down on the couch and say, "Doctor, I can't help myself. I must go to games. I must follow Henry Aaron. I must see home run number 715." "I don't have to go out there, I go because I want to," he says. During the fall, in that time period when all the sports overlap, Drago might go to five or six games a week. "A couple of basketball games, two football games on the weekend and as many baseball games as I can get to see." He doesn't view attending that many games a week as compulsive. "I don't know, maybe I'm weird, but I don't regard that as a lot of games.

"Oh, sure, I appreciate that other people might think it's weird. But I don't know . . . I like the action. If there's something going on, I want to be there and . . . I don't know . . . it's difficult to say. I mean, maybe, maybe there's something I'm looking for I haven't found. I don't know."

What Drago has not found at his games are women. Sports, Drago understands, is a little bit too important to get bogged down in socializing. "You could say that going to all the games has been a little disruptive to my social life. About two years ago, I had a situation where I had somebody who wanted to go with me to all the games, and that was no problem. But I had another situation where I had a type of thing where I couldn't get involved to the extent this girl wanted to get involved. Uh——uh——I told her, I just gotta do my games and I just can't put in that much time with you. So I've sort of given up taking girls to games. Half the time they're in the bathroom when Hank is batting. It's really a hopeless situation. I guess maybe in a weak moment I might take one again. But I've got something bigger at stake."

There is, of course, a very thin line between "something bigger at stake" and a compulsion. He says, and it is obviously true, that he doesn't go to all the games to compensate for a dull, repetitive life. "I could probably eliminate sports from my life," he says, "eliminate it one hundred percent——I wouldn't want to, but I could——and never go to another ball game, and I don't think there'd be too many dull moments in my life."

Chris Drago goes into his bedroom, brings out a long cardboard box that is filled with his stub collection. Drago estimates that he has about 400 stubs, but some are doubles. He collects the stubs every time he goes to a game. It started with him a few years ago when he needed to facilitate his hawking. "Hawking" is the term Drago uses to describe how he gets into games, frequently for nothing, always for less than the official price. "I just couldn't go to all the games I want to go to if I had to pay," he says. So he gets to his games two and three hours early, walks around the stadium, checks out the market and tries to hawk tickets. There is usually someone around who is stuck with an extra and will give it away or sell it cheaply. There are times—"oh, the Auburn-Houston game"—when even though he already had bought reserved tickets Drago hawked seats before the game anyway, "just to see if I could."

The talk returns to Henry Aaron, to the Braves, to home run number 715 again. Eight months before the season had begun, Drago had already written to every team in the National League, asking for their schedules, requesting their ticket plans. "If I'm alive and he hasn't hit 715, I'll be at the park," Drago is saying.

A hypothetical situation is set up: Drago is at the park; Aaron hits number 715; Drago reaches over with his butterfly net and catches number 715. There is a man, in Cincinnati, Drago believes, who says he will offer $50,000 for the ball that becomes number 715. What does Drago, the man with a 37-cent baseball glove, do?

"I wouldn't want to keep it, not if Henry didn't want me to," he says. "The first thing I'd do is go to Hank and see what he wanted me to do with it. I'd ask him first. I'm not going to run to the highest bidder. Sure I'd *like* to have it, but it's *his*."

What about meeting Hank on another occasion? "Well, obviously I'd like to meet him. But at this stage he's got enough trouble with everybody trying to meet him. I figure, what does he want to be bothered by one more guy? I don't want to pester him. Like I said, what does he want to be bothered by one more jerk?"

He's just one more guy, one more guy who likes sports. Eliminate sports from his life? Well, he'd rather not. It's not *that* important, he's just another guy who likes it. Drago is gassing the eight-dollar Buick, pushing it up the hill, past the fast-food franchise stands that surround Memphis. Drago will be leaving Memphis in a few days, after the Liberty Bowl, to go down to the Sugar Bowl basketball tournament. Then he'll be going to the Sugar Bowl football game.

"You know," he is saying, "I don't really know why anybody would want to read about me. I'm not the biggest fan in the world. I'm not the greatest fan in the world. There's this guy who goes to all the Alabama football games, I mean all of them. I don't think he's missed but three in fifteen years. And at the beginning of each season he has this thing he calls the meat pole. It's a great big, long pole that he extends, a telescopic thing. And at the top of it he's got this great big banner that says ' 'Bama Meat Pole.' And on each section he's got a banner on it for each team 'Bama beats. And after each game he parades around the stadium with it. Well, it's not too exciting at first. But by the time he's got about ten pennants on the damn thing and then he gets the cheerleaders to run with it, you know. . . . Now that man, he's a fan. That's a real fan. Me, I'm just a normal guy about it."

THE CRAZIEST ONES OF ALL: HILDA, SHORTY AND OTHER BUMMERS

8

LEAVE US GO ROOT FOR THE DODGERS, RODGERS

Murgatroyd Darcy, a broad from Canarsie,
Went 'round with a fellow named Rodge.
At dancing a rumba or jitterbug numbah
You couldn't beat Rodge—'twas his dodge.
The pair danced together throughout the cold weather
But when the trees blossomed again
Miss Murgatroyd Darcy, the belle of Canarsie,
To Rodgers would sing this refrain:

Leave us go root for the Dodgers, Rodgers,
They're playing ball under lights.
Leave us cut out all the juke jernts, Rodgers,
Where we've been wastin' our nights.
Dancin' the shag or the rumba is silly
When we can be rooting for Adolf Camilli,
So leave us go root for the Dodgers, Rodgers,
Them Dodgers is my gallant knights.

—Dan Daniel, sports editor,
New York Daily Mirror.

There has simply never been a group of fans like the fans of the Brooklyn Dodgers. This is a point beyond debate. We will not brook contradiction here. There is no question.

Don't go bringing up Green Bay Packer fans or Miami Dolphin fans. It's just not pertinent to mention the fans of the Boston Bruins or Montreal Canadiens. Notre Dame fans? University of Texas adherents? Mets boosters, Cardinal cheerers,

100 GOD SAVE THE PLAYERS

Pittsburgh—Pirate or Steeler—partisans? They just won't do. They don't measure up.

All of those teams have had fanatical followers, people who would go to any lengths to show their love and devotion. They were—*are*—great groups of fans, interesting, varied, long-standing, widespread. But they were not the Brooklyn Dodgers fans. They may all tie for second. The fans of the Brooklyn Dodgers were the most fanatical, frenzied, outlandish, loony, wonderful group ever to form under the banner of one team. They are number one.

If you severed the borough of Brooklyn from the rest of New York, Brooklyn would be the third largest city in the country. It is a world unto itself. Separated from Manhattan by the sickly waters of the East River, and from Queens, the only borough to which it is physically attached, by a world of attitudes, Brooklyn has always considered itself separate and distinct. It did not join with the other four boroughs to form the modern New York City until 1898. And when it did join, there was a great uproar. Most of the Brooklynites didn't want consolidation. Brooklyn had its own hotels and its own downtown. If the rest of New York had Central Park, Brooklyn had Prospect Park, planned by the same man and considered superior in design. If Manhattan had the lights of Broadway, Brooklyn had the lights of Coney Island. So New York had their Giants and Yankees. Brooklyn had its Dodgers.

Brooklyn also had much that the rest of New York lacked. In the middle of the most highly urbanized area in the country, it was almost a bucolic retreat. It was a borough of neighborhoods, each with a distinct identity. Through the low-profile buildings, wide avenues and quaint place names, Brooklyn retained the feel of the days when it was Dutch farmland. Unlike the rest of New York, Brooklyn hadn't melted down its neighborhoods, and its people, to form one large, unwieldly, ineffectively homogenized world.

Yet, with all they had, Brooklynites were resentful of the boroughs across the water. Somehow they were like stepchildren of the big city, shunted off, banished upstairs. New York had the glittering skyline and the glamor and received all the publicity. New York had the fancy women and sophisticated men. New York was the center, the place to which the people gravitated, while Brooklyn made sure New York's trains were on time and the refrigerators worked. While New Yorkers were smooth, Brooklynites had funny accents—Greenpoint was "Greenpernt"—and were the butt of jokes. A comedian only had to mention the word "Brooklyn" and people started to laugh. In 1898 Brooklyn had submerged its own distinctive identity into New York's and it wasn't happy about it.

"When I got to Brooklyn in 1939," Red Barber, the broadcaster, has written, "resentment was still there, and it was a genuine resentment. These were the masses, subjects of the glittering city across the river. Brooklyn had a borowide inferiority complex."

The complex extended to sports. Across the river in Manhattan were the Giants, the team of John McGraw, Christy Mathewson, Bill Terry. The Giants were the colossus of the National League, had been almost from its inception. Up in the Bronx were the Yankees, the team of Ruth and Gehrig and DiMaggio, the automatons, the colossus of all baseball.

Yes, Brooklyn had the Dodgers, but, lacking stars, they were weak sisters, poor relations. But they were Brooklyn's. The Dodgers were bums, sure, but they were *our* bums. Smile when you say it.

102   GOD SAVE THE PLAYERS

Perhaps is was the long-term incompetence of the Dodgers and the inferiority feelings of the Brooklynites that made the Dodger fans so special. "The fanaticism of the Dodger fans grew on pain," Red Barber believes. The Dodger fans weren't front-runners. They weren't demanding. They would just as soon heckle their own as they would the opposition. Through the pain and frustration of the bad years the fanaticism built up. Each loss seemed to be an affront from the Manhattans of the world, and it made the fans that much more fanatical. Just wait. "Wait Till Next Year." It became an anthem.

Brooklyn had been home to a professional baseball team since 1883. At one time, late in the 19th Century when there were three leagues, Brooklyn had a team in all three. The team that was to become the Dodgers was at various times called the Atlantics, the Superbas, the Robins and once, for a few years, the Bridegrooms, because six members of the team had just gotten married. The tradition of Dodger fandom is almost as old as the club. Early in the century, when the team was still playing at Washington Park, rooters would go up on the rooftops of Ginney Flats, which were apartments across the street. From there, and from the fire escapes, they would hurl spears made of umbrella ribs at opposing outfielders.

But the fans didn't truly come into their glory until the team moved into Ebbets Field in 1913. This was what they had been waiting for. Ebbets Field was made for fans—unlike today when new stadiums are made for the tax accountants. "When you had a box seat at Ebbets Field," Barber says, "you were practically playing the infield."

Known as the "laugh house of baseball," Ebbets Field made its own specific contributions

HILDA, SHORTY AND OTHER BUMMERS 103

to the loony atmosphere. On the very day the stadium started operations and the first game was scheduled to be played, the gates were thrown open—except no one could find the key to the bleacher gates. There were also no ticket sellers on the job until after one o'clock. No one had told them to arrive any earlier. Finally, when the owners of the new stadium had marched, along with Shannon's Band, to the center-field flagpole to hoist the flag, it was discovered that there was no flag to hoist.

Ebbets Field was centrally located, almost in the geographical middle of Brooklyn, and consequently almost everybody would walk to the park. "On any given night," says Tommy Holmes, who covered the team for many years for the *Brooklyn Eagle*, "half of the thirty or thirty-two thousand fans there could get home in fifteen minutes. It was the hub of several neighborhoods. It had two subways, three or four different streetcar lines. I'll bet there were days when ten thousand of the fifteen thousand there could walk to and from the park. It was in a residential area. All around, for a couple of miles, there was nothing but homes."

It was the neighborhood meeting place, a place where friends, close and long-lost, could get together. You'd walk from your house and you'd meet a few of the other guys on the way and you'd all just end up at Ebbets Field.

Ebbets, particularly compared to today's mammoth, impersonal parks, was tiny and personal. Only Wrigley Field in Chicago and Fenway Park in Boston are survivors of the species. The normal capacity for Ebbets was 28,000. For the big weekend games, 9000 temporary bleacher seats were added. With those extra seats, people sitting in the outfield had to stand to see, and that would block the view of those at the extreme ends of the grandstands. So *they* would stand up. Before half the game was over, just about everybody in the park was on their feet. These were not sedentary fans.

Although the people were there, in full voice, from the beginning, they did not really blossom as the true loonies they were to become until the 1930s. In fact, in the Twenties, when the Dodgers were among the worst clubs in baseball, the fans, though loud and normally eccentric, did not support them in nearly the manner to which the team would later become accustomed.

Then came the Thirties and the daffiness boys. And the daffiness fans. The daffiness boys were the Dodgers of the era—not the best team in the league, not the worst either. Just the weirdest. They did crazy, inexplicable things, like having players triple into a double play or having three players wind up on the same base.

The daffiness boys brought the Dodger fans out of the closet. As Red Barber says, "There were nearly three million people in Brooklyn then, and if every one of them wasn't rooting for the Dodgers, every one *seemed* to be."

But some rooted harder—or at least differently —than others.

There was Robert Joyce. On July 12, 1938, Joyce, as was his custom, was among the usual group of neighborhood customers at Pat Diamond's Bar and Grill on Ninth Avenue in Brooklyn. The Dodgers had lost that afternoon to the hated Giants, and as usual the talk around the bar was of the game. While everyone bemoaned the fate of the Dodgers, Joyce just stared into his beer. William Diamond, the son of the proprietor, started to have a little fun with Joyce, who took all Dodger losses with such dreadful seriousness.

"The Dodgers," Diamond playfully called out.

HILDA, SHORTY AND OTHER BUMMERS 105

"Whoever first called them bums was right. Don't you think so, Frank?"

Frank Krug, down the bar, was in from Albany to spend his vacation with relatives. Krug was a Giant fan. "It takes the Giants to show them up as bums," he said to Joyce. "Why don't you get wise, Bob, and root for a real team?"

The teasing continued. Suddenly, Joyce straightened up, his eyes afire. "Shut up," he screamed. "Shut up, you bastards. You lay off the Dodgers, you dirty bastards!"

Everyone else started to laugh.

"You don't mean to say you're mad at us boys, do you?" William Diamond finally said to Joyce. "Don't be a jerk," Krug decided to add.

"A jerk!" Joyce screamed hysterically. "I'll show you who's a jerk."

Robert Joyce rushed out of the bar. Three minutes later he returned, carrying a gun. He shot Krug through the head, killing him. He shot Diamond in the stomach, seriously wounding him. Then he ran.

When the police finally caught up with Robert Joyce, he was sobbing uncontrollably. "They shouldn't have taunted me about the Dodgers," he cried to the police.

There was Eddie Betan. He was an apartment superintendent, a loud, friendly man who was there at Ebbets Field from the Twenties on. He always carried a shrill whistle in his pocket. Each game, Betan would pick out a particular Dodger player and start to yell at him and continuously blow the whistle at him. If, say, Whitlow Wyatt was pitching, Betan would stand behind home plate shouting, "Whit, Whit," and blow the whistle. He wouldn't stop calling and whistling and waving until Whit would wave back and acknowledge him. Then Betan would stop.

There was the Flatbush native who was on

death row in Massachusetts State Prison. He was there for the murder of a Boston policeman. On April 21, 1941, he was taken out of his cell for the long walk to the electric chair. As he sat in the chair after being plugged in, he turned to the guards and said: "One last thing. Did the Bums beat the Giants today?"

There was Fierce Jack Pierce. He sat in a box seat right behind the Dodger dugout. He carried with him an air machine that could blow up balloons. He also had a thing for Cookie Lavagetto. Every time Cookie would get up to hit, Fierce Jack Pierce would blow up a balloon and float it into the air. As far as anyone can remember, this went on for six or seven years.

There was Frank Germano. If not for his love of the Dodgers, Frank Germano would've been a free man. It happened in September 1940. The Dodgers were playing Cincinnati, and Leo Durocher, the Brooklyn manager, had been riding the umpire all afternoon. In fact, all the Dodgers were riding umpire George Magerkurth. The game ended and Magerkurth was walking off the field when suddenly, out of the stands, came a burly figure hurtling the guard rail. He ran right to Magerkurth, threw himself at the umpire and started a very professional mugging. Magerkurth, who had once been a heavyweight boxer, was defenseless against the inspired onslaught. Some of the other umpires and some Dodgers eventually pulled the fan off. He was taken by the police down to the Flatbush courthouse for arraignment. There, waiting for Frank Germano, was a parole officer with a warrant for his arrest on a charge of parole violation. Frank Germano, who had previously been a perfect parolee, was returned to New York's West Coxsackie Vocational Institution.

There was the singing newsboy, age about 60,

who had his newsstand right near the park. Instead of shouting "extry, extry," which was the fashionable cry of the times, every night the singing newsboy would chant about the fortunes of his Dodgers. In the late Forties, when Dodger President Branch Rickey was unloading a lot of old veterans like Wyatt and Dolph Camilli, the singing newsboy started his mournful chant: "Camilli went, an' his heart was broke," he wailed. "Oh, Rickey, what you done to our pal."

There was Tony Grimeli, who owned a bar not far from the stadium. In 1941, when the Dodgers started to make their first serious run for a pennant in 20 years, Grimeli's bar offered to anyone who paid three dollars before the game all the beer he wanted, free transportation to Ebbets, a free reserved seat in back of first base, free return transportation and then more free beer for as long as he could sip. It was mentioned to Grimeli that this seemed to be a marvelous way to lose a lot of money. "Nah," Grimeli answered. "At the bar, only the beer is free, and I know these people. The Dodgers make them very excited and when they come back here after the game and start to argue, they forget about the beer and buy whiskey."

There was Bill Boylan, a milkman, who when game time arrived used to tie his horse and wagon (it was that long ago) to the gate outside the park and then go in. Boylan would go directly onto the field and pitch batting practice to Babe Herman. Herman, who had been in a slump, believed that this practice was the only way he could get out of it.

There was the Reverend Benney J. Benson of the Brooklyn Dutch Reformed Church, who held a service to pray for a pennant for the Dodgers on the steps of the Brooklyn Borough Hall.

There was the priest, who in 1952 asked his

parishioners—and the entire borough—to pray for Gil Hodges to get a hit during the World Series. Hodges, then the Dodger first baseman, still went the entire series without a hit.

There was the multitude of fans who have remained anonymous, like the one berating the Dodgers in front of Toots Shor, the well-known drinker. The fan had been calling Dolph Camilli a bum all afternoon. Finally, Shor couldn't take any more of it. He leaned over and tapped the fan on the shoulder. "I wish you wouldn't call Camilli a bum," he said. "He's a friend of mine and a very nice guy. If you knew him you wouldn't call him a bum."

"All right," the fan said, grudgingly. "If he's a friend of yours, I'll lay off him."

Dixie Walker was the next hitter, and the fan started in on him. "You bum. Put that bat down and let somebody hit that can hit."

Shor tapped the fan on the shoulder again. The fan whirled around. "Is Walker your friend, too?" he yelled.

Shor nodded.

"Are all these bums your friends?"

Shor nodded again.

The fan got up and started across the aisle, headed for a seat in another section. "I'm gettin' the hell away from you," he screamed back. "You ain't gonna spoil my afternoon."

There was, as Tommy Holmes remembers him, "a mystery guy, in the Thirties, who was around for only one summer." No one ever found out his name, he wouldn't give it out, he didn't want any publicity. He would sit alone, on weekdays, never near any crowds. He'd sit by third base, at the very top of the upper deck, with his trumpet. Between innings, between *all* innings, he would play the trumpet. He would play popular music and he played it quite well. He was just practicing, he told people. Ebbets Field was his practice studio. But he never played while the game was on, because he didn't want to detract from it.

There was a man in the late Twenties who was referred to by a newspaperman as "The Spirit of Brooklyn." He always sat under the press box and would scream out, over and over again, "You bums you! You bums you!" That was when the team was doing badly. When the team was doing *very* badly it was "Youse bums youse!" Or maybe the first way was singular and the second one plural. Possibly—no one really knows for sure—this was how the Dodgers came to be known as the "Bums." Or maybe not.

In addition to all these individuals, there was one group called the Dodger Sym-phony. "Remember, the accent is on the phony," reminds Red Barber, who coined the name. The band was led by Shorty Laurice, a very small man who was a truck driver. When the games started, Shorty would park his truck in front of the stadium and come in. He would put on his silk hat, which was labeled "Our Bums," join with the other members of the band, all dressed in tattered tuxedoes, and they would parade through the stands, playing.

Well, they wouldn't play, exactly. "They *couldn't* play any music," Barber remembers. "They didn't know any notes." What they would do was make a lot of noise with their instruments. "They were terrible, but they were nice and noisy and good-natured."

Shorty Laurice proudly boasted that the Symphony was "the worst band in the world." Shorty didn't actually play in the band all the time. At first he played the bass drum, but then he found a midget named Jo Jo, the only person he could find smaller than himself, and Jo Jo would carry around the bass drum and beat on it. Jo Jo, who weighed 40 pounds, liked to smoke a cigar while he was playing. Once Branch Rickey saw him smoking and told Shorty, "That child shouldn't be up this late, nor should he be smoking cigars."

"Child, me eyebrow," Shorty eloquently replied. "He's older'n you are, Branch."

Utilizing his ever-present megaphone and waving wildly to the band, Shorty led them in attempting to irritate the opposition. When an opposing hitter struck out, the Symphony accompanied the batter back to the bench with an infuriating galoomph-galoomph for each step. When the hitter sat down, there was a clash of cymbals. If the hitter tried to confuse everybody by going to get a drink instead of sitting down, the band would loudly play "How Dry I Am."

"It drives them nuts," Shorty used to say with a very wide grin.

These were all marvelously loony fans, outlandish, completely devoted, passionate. And then there was Hilda, Hilda Chester, Hilda of the cowbell and the Brooklynese and the sign saying "Hilda Is Here." Hilda, as she and everyone else described her, "the first lady of Flatbush."

The woman at the desk of the Park Nursing Home, in Rockaway Park, New York, kept repeating, "I'm sure she won't want to talk, not about baseball, not about those days. She doesn't like to talk about them anymore. She doesn't even like to talk about them to us."

She doesn't like to talk with anyone from the outside, the woman went on. "And least of all about baseball. Something happened, I don't know what," the woman said.

Miss Chester had told them not to let anyone in to see her, she said. But yes, Miss Chester would pick up the phone.

HILDA, SHORTY AND OTHER BUMMERS

"The old days with the Brooklyn Dodgers, no, that's out," said the "First Lady of Flatbush" over the phone. "Absolutely out. Out. Since nineteen fifty . . . three."

The voice was crackly and nasal. Hilda Chester has been at the home for over four years and is close to 75 years old now. But just like in the old days, she is still very stubborn.

"Oh," she said, and the "oh" lasted for a few beats, "I don't know. I never even think of it. The old days. I never give it a thought. No. I don't want to talk about it. No. No. No. I'm a hundred percent positive. No. No. No. No particular reason. It's all over, that's it. That's the only reason. I'm sorry. That's all I have to say. I'm sorry. But it's all over. That's it. I'm sorry. I'm sorry."

It is over, but it still lives. The images are that strong.

Hilda Chester started going to Dodger games in the Thirties. By the Forties she was already widely known as "The First Lady." Her voice was exceptionally loud and classically Brooklynese in its tones. "You know me," she'd say to people. "Hilda wit' th' bell. Ain't it trillin'? Home wuz never like dis, Mac."

She would always sit in the bleachers. At first she started bringing a frying pan and beating that for her heroes. Then she switched to ringing a set of brass bells. Sometime in the Forties she injured her wrist in a fall, and her doctor suggested she exercise it. That led her to her famous cowbell. She would ring the cowbell every time the Dodgers rallied or every time they needed encouragement.

Eventually the management took notice of her. It was somewhat difficult to avoid taking notice of someone who was ringing a cowbell in your bleachers every day. A Dodger executive went out to the bleachers to her one day. "Hilda," he said, "wouldn't you like to sit in the grandstand, right back of the dugout? I'll have a place reserved every day if you would."

Hilda replied with a look of withering scorn. "Did any of those plush-seat bums come near me when I was in the hospital?" she asked. "Not one. But the ballplayers did, and they sent me cards and letters and flowers, and the boys and girls out here were dropping in all the time. No, sir, I'll stay right here, thank you. And anyway, I can't relax in them fancy seats."

As the Dodgers became an important factor in the National League, Hilda became prominent. Her picture appeared in newspapers all over the country. She was interviewed on radio. She became the symbol of the Dodgers.

When Hilda followed her team to Philadelphia, with her bell and her voice, her reputation preceded her. Bob Carpenter, the Phillies' president, asked Pete Adelis, "the Iron Lung of Shibe Park," to have a chance at her. Carpenter obtained the seat next to Hilda for the top Philadelphia voice, and the shouting match of the decade was on. Reports vary as to the outcome.

When Hollywood made the *Jackie Robinson Story*, they included a very Hilda Chesterish figure in the movie. Every time the director wanted to show the crowd reaction to something Jackie had done, the camera focused on a raucous, middle-aged, heavy-set woman wearing large-framed glasses. Her voice, which dominated the scenes, was constitutionally unable to not garble the words. Every time something good happened to the Dodgers, the character would nudge everyone sitting near her. The woman in the movie was never identified, but identification wasn't necessary. Hilda was that well known.

HILDA, SHORTY AND OTHER BUMMERS 113

Which was probably her downfall. "She began as a genuine fan," Red Barber remembers, "but when she got all the write-ups and the radio mentions, she began to take it all too seriously." That was when she started unfurling her "Hilda Is Here" banner. At the end of the Forties, when Leo Durocher, always one of Hilda's favorites, moved over to the Giants, Hilda moved with him. She abandoned Brooklyn, left the Bums. She remained vaguely prominent for a few more years, but it was never the same. The same fire wasn't there.

It soon was the same for all the Dodgers fans. The fire went out for them in 1957. The Dodgers left Brooklyn. The glory of Flatbush and Canarsie and Brownsville and Park Slope left Brooklyn for Los Angeles, which doesn't even have any neighborhoods.

It will never be the same. Where else could a pennant-winning parade—in 1941—draw over a million people? It was the biggest parade, old-timers said, since the Fourteenth Zouaves and the Twenty-Third Regiment returned from the Civil War. Where else could a lowly haberdasher, whose major claim to fame was a sign with his name challenging the players to "Hit Sign, Win Suit," become borough president? Where else could the ball-park announcer, the illustrious Tex Rickard, announce, " 'Tension, puhleeze. A child has been found lost"?

Where else? Shea Stadium is in the borough of Queens, due north of Brooklyn. It is maybe ten miles from where Ebbets Field was, perhaps 20 minutes on the Brooklyn-Queen's Expressway. If the spirit of Brooklyn, of the Dodger fans, lives anywhere, it lives here at the home of the Mets.

From 1957 until 1962, New York had only one baseball team, the Yankees. Although they were

114 GOD SAVE THE PLAYERS

still winning pennants then, they did not excite the town. They were too efficient, lacked humanity. Hell, they just won too much. Anyway, New York was a National League city. During the five years when the Yankees were the only wheel in town, their attendance did not markedly increase. The two million people who had been going to see the Dodgers and Giants did not switch over to the Yankees.

Instead they waited. Some might go down to Philadelphia to see the two old clubs when they made their eastern swings, but most of the old fans left baseball temporarily and waited.

Then, in 1962, the Mets. This was what they had been waiting for. Maybe it was not high-quality, but it was National League baseball. And who could better empathize and sympathize with the worst team in the history of baseball than Dodger fans? They knew—and could love—bums when they saw them.

It was the Dodger fans who gave the Met fans an identity. They were still competing against the Yankees, could still be the downtrodden underdogs. Every year, the Mets would have their largest crowds when the Dodgers would come back to town to play. Even known Dodger hangers-on could be seen hanging around the Mets, people like Looie Kleppel, sometimes referred to as "dirty Looie" because he looked like he was born and lived in a ragged old topcoat.

The Met fans were called "the new breed." The old breed, of course, were the Dodger fans.

When the Met fans rioted and almost tore up Shea Stadium—and the Cincinnati Reds—during the 1973 play-offs, solid citizens, newspaper editorialists, baseball officials and Cincinnatians were shocked. This was unspeakable. Why, something like this had never happened before.

"People do things like this today and they

get away with it," said Sparky Anderson, the Cincinnati manager. "Nobody seems to care anymore. Maybe they are all on marijuana."

But in 1941, when thousands of Dodger fans descended on Shibe Park before the Dodgers played the Phillies, brushed cops and ushers out of their way, swirled out onto the field during batting practice and forced it to be canceled, no one knew much about marijuana.

So, maybe the whole borough was high. They could've been getting it directly from the water system back in the Thirties and Forties. Or they were growing it in Prospect Park. That had to be the reason. As close as the Mets fans come to recapturing the spirit of it all, there has never really been a bunch like the fans of the Brooklyn Dodgers. It wuz trillin', Mac.

RICHARD NIXON, OL' NUMBER TWELVE

9

It is Memorial Day, 1957, at old Griffith Stadium, Washington, D.C. The Yankees are playing a holiday doubleheader against the Senators. It is between games, the time for rest, relaxation, hot dogs. Bob Wolff, the Senators broadcaster, is walking through the stands, looking for his between games radio interview.

"Hi, everybody, this is Bob Wolff with your pregame preview brought to you by Todds and Amana air conditioners. Amana—the first big name in home air conditioning to let you match your air conditioner with the decor of your home. See Todds about the space-saving, central-cooling Amana air conditioner.

"On this pregame show I thought we'd do something new for a change. As you know, we've heard so much from the ballplayers, and the coaches and officials and the managers, I thought today just at random I'd go down and let you hear from some of the folks who are gathered here at Griffith Stadium to watch this big Memorial Day doubleheader. So I just sauntered down here, down in the first deck, and I think that I'll ask this first gentleman here who has been watching the ball game how he's enjoying the game. Sir, how'd you like the first game today?"

"Well, of course, being a Washington fan, I thought it was great. And, uh, I particularly, of course, like everybody else, got a big thrill out of that homer Jim Lemon hit against the wind into those left-field seats."

"Well, these boys, you know, have been playing inspired ball. Have you had a chance to see many other games this season?"

"Well, I came out opening night—opening day—I saw the president throw the ball out that day, and Washington, as you recall, lost to the Yankees I believe—uh—it was a pretty good game though. Otherwise, I've been seeing it on television. I've seen you, as a matter of fact, too, but as you know we haven't done too well. But I did see the game the other day on TV which started this winning streak—that is, the second game of the Baltimore doubleheader the other day."

"I see you brought your daughter with you today."

"Yes, and she has never seen a baseball game until today except on television, so this was a lucky day for her to see the winning game."

"Well, that's terrific."

"She also got a baseball signed by Cookie Lavegetto, so she's pretty happy."

"Isn't that wonderful! I see you are sitting pretty near the playing field, so that is just great. What'd you think of the pitching in the first game?"

"Well, of course, for Washington it was just great and we all know Washington's been having some tough luck with its pitching. I was particularly glad to see Pascual finally beat the Yankees, as I understand he's never beaten them before. And, of course, that relief pitching was tops, too, and against the Yankees this was something."

"Are you originally from Washington, sir?"

"No, I'm a Californian. I was and still am."

"Well, some of our boys on the team come from California."

"I just heard that several of them did. Lou Berberet I understand is. Rocky Bridges came from California. And then Bob Usher's been playing in San Diego I think. And they all did pretty well today, too."

"Well, that's great that you can be here all the way from California. Have you done much traveling around the country?"

"Yes, I've been in most of the forty-eight states at one time or another. And also I've traveled a bit abroad in the last few years."

"So you've had a chance to see quite a bit of baseball?"

"Well, not as much as I would like. I catch it whenever I can, but usually I must say I see it on television."

"Did you have a chance to do any playing of sports yourself?"

"Well, I'll tell ya. I s'pose one of the reasons I like both baseball and football is that I went out and never made the team. So I like to watch others that can do it."

"I see. Well, how long have you been here in the nation's capital? For some time?"

"Well, off and on, I've been here about ten years."

"Oh, well, you're practically a native right here now."

"Practically a Washingtonian by this time."

"I see. What sort of work do you do sir?"

"I work for the government."

"For the government?"

"Yes, yes, for the government."

"Oh?"

"My boss is President Eisenhower."

"Your boss is President Eisenhower? What sort of work do you do, sir?

"Well, I'm the vice-president."

"Ladies and gentlemen, our guest has been the vice-president of the United States, Vice-President Nixon. . . . We always give our guest these Countess Farah neckties."

"This is fine. I'm always in need of ties because I usually have to wear one."

There are some who believe that Richard Nixon is a nouveau sports fan, that as president he has felt it incumbent on himself to be interested in what he perceived the American people were interested in: sports. This theory is usually coupled with the appreciation of Nixon as Machiavellian politician. Spectating is the great outlet, interest, emotional involvement of his beloved silent majority. Nixon can show he is one of them, can give their passions official endorsement, by embracing sports himself. There is also the belief that Nixon is trying to involve the people in games, and consequently take their minds off pressing—and embarrassing—national and international issues. Nothing controversial about sports. Sports is healthy, American, patriotic. No one can blame the president, can disagree with him, for liking sports.

This theory is, however, just not true. Anyone who would go, unsolicitedly, privately, to a Washington Senators game—a doubleheader!—in the 1950s, anyone who could care about Lou Berberet, is entitled to be called a fan. Richard Nixon is an honest-to-goodness fan.

Richard Nixon, the thirty-seventh president of the United States, enjoys being referred to as the "nation's number-one sports fan." But he is not the first president to be a sports fan, nor the first to be called the "nation's number-one sports fan." It seems to come with the job.

William Howard Taft enjoyed baseball, and was the first president to throw out the first ball at an opening game. Abe Lincoln like to bowl, and to watch others bowl. Dwight Eisenhower, as we all know, was interested in golf. John

Kennedy, although he preferred participant sports, enjoyed watching both football and baseball. And Nixon's immediate predecessor, Lyndon Johnson, enjoyed football, although he did have certain qualms about the cosmic importance of it all.

"It's a great spectacle," Johnson once said, "but I am not sure it gives an accurate picture of America. To see some of our best-educated boys spending an afternoon knocking each other down, while thousands cheer them on, hardly gives an ideal picture of a peace-loving nation."

Richard Nixon believes both that it is an ideal picture and that we are a peace-loving nation. He may be half right. It is an ideal picture to him. It's clean-cut all-American youth coming face-to-shinguard with crisis and overcoming obstacles through perseverance and determination. Richard Nixon, the quintessential self-made man, who has seen his entire public life as a series of crises which he has had to overcome, believes that "in life, as well as in sports, politics and business, what really makes a team or a country is, when it has lost one, it doesn't lose its spirit." He enjoys the battle of sport. And like other prominent men who spend their lives dealing with ambiguous problems and unclear choices, he enjoys sports because they are controlled, definitive. Self-made young men are achieving self-made victories.

It is too facile to explain the spectating of the president, 1968–1974, as identification or as the yearnings of a middle-aged man who never made the team and now must get his athletic victories vicariously. Surely the president of the United States must have had enough thrilling moments and victories of his own.

Perhaps the spectating of the president is more understandable in view of Nixon's suburban

RICHARD NIXON, OL' NUMBER TWELVE 121

background. Nixon is the first president who is truly suburban, in upbringing, outlook, enthusiasms. He was brought up in Whittier, California, a suburb of Los Angeles, which is like being brought up in a suburb of a suburb. The suburban man is, almost by definition, an observer, an interloper, a person on the periphery. He is involved, but not viscerally. That is also the definition of a spectator.

President Nixon has been a spectator almost since the beginning. At Whittier College he went out for the fooball team all four years he was in the school. He was only able to make the team, however, during his freshman year. Only 11 men turned out for the team that year. The last three years he was used as cannon fodder by the varsity. "I got into a game once when we were so far behind it didn't matter," he told the National Football Foundation dinner in 1969. "I even got into one against Southern California, when we were also so far behind it didn't matter. One of the reasons the coach didn't put me in was because I didn't know the plays. There was a good reason for that. It wasn't because I wasn't smart enough. I knew the enemy's plays. I played them all week long. Believe me, nobody in the Southern California conference knew Occidental's or Pomona's plays better than I did."

Ol' number 12 at Whittier never did get his varsity letter there. He had to wait 35 years, until 1969, to receive it. It was given to him by his old coach, Chief Newman, at a testimonial dinner. Newman also gave the president-elect a wooden bench, the very one Nixon had sat on during his playing days. Newman seems to have been a major influence on Nixon. He was apparently a man of stringent attitudes, a man who understood that the world was black and white and that you played to win. He was a man who

122 GOD SAVE THE PLAYERS

could apply the finite logic of sports to the infinite illogic of life.

At the pro-football Hall of Fame induction ceremonies in 1969, the president recalled his old coach in the most glowing terms he could muster. He compared him to Vince Lombardi. "Chief Newman was a man much like Vince Lombardi because he impressed on his players the importance of being a good loser, but also stressed you've got to hate to lose. You have to get off the floor and fight again. I had to lose before I won."

Nixon has carried the logic of sports with him throughout his political career——and the metaphor of sports, too. He is the one who popularized the term "game plan" for what you do in Southeast Asia, or in an energy crisis, or a domestic scandal. The code name the president chose for himself during the first Vietnam negotiations was "quarterback." He is always "pitching" a proposal, "making an end run," hanging in there when "the count's three and two." Nixon considers himself "the quarterback" of the government.

"My own career," he has said, carrying the metaphor a little bit further than it will go, "was sort of a fourth-quarter finish and a pass perhaps in the last thirty seconds to win."

But metaphor isn't enough. Nixon seems to get even greater pleasure out of his role as *active* superfan. That might be why he chose an old Michigan lineman, Gerry Ford, to be his new vice-president. That must be the reason why he's always on the phone to somebody in sports.

Since becoming president he has called or written George Allen, Marty Liquori, Jack Nicklaus, Ralph Houk, Bob Devaney, Henry Aaron, Johnny Majors, George Allen, Harmon Killebrew, Vince Lombardi, Pedro Ramos, John

Wooden, Bear Bryant, Frank Gifford, Orville Moody, Reggie Jackson, George Allen, Hank Stram, Len Dawson, Joan Payson, Arnold Palmer, Darrell Royal, George Allen, Ted Williams, Don Shula, Sonny Jurgensen, the United States and Rumanian Davis Cup teams, the Washington and Lee High School rowing team, Billy Kilmer, Danny Murtaugh, Earl Weaver, Joseph Danzansky and George Allen.

The calls have not always been welcome. Sometimes the recipients have even been, well, nonplussed. Billy Kilmer, the occasional Redskin quarterback, once said about the president's calls: "He's really hurting us. He calls all the time. I think I'm going to ask George Allen to tell the president not to talk about the game until after we've played it."

When Nixon called Miami Dolphin coach Don Shula at one in the morning the week before a Super Bowl game, Shula said, "I thought it was some idiot calling at that time. Then I found out it was the president of the United States."

There are other athletes, not necessarily recipients of the calls, who also don't appreciate the president's smother-loving involvement with sports. Larry Csonka, the Dolphins fullback, has complained that "President Nixon may identify with football players, but I don't identify with him, and I haven't met a player yet who does. The man upsets me with his role as superjock. Here he is, the one man in the world who has, at his fingertips, all the information and influence to make a lot of people's lives better. But what's he doing calling football players on the telephone and giving pep talks to teams? It just brainwashes people more, makes people think football is a lot more important to them than it really is. He's either hung-up on the violence or else he's pulling off a master con job on a lot of sports fans. He's implying that he's one of them and he's hoping to get their votes in return."

Dave Meggyesy, the erstwhile pro linebacker and nouveau radical who doesn't like football any more than he likes Republicans, finds Nixon as spectator indicative of troubles all around. "It is no accident," Meggyesy says, "that the number-one football freak in the country is Richard Nixon. The Mitchell-Agnew-Nixon mentality is what football is all about."

In 1971, when Nixon unexpectedly drove out to a Redskin practice to mingle and advise, interior lineman Ray Shonke walked away from the president, refusing to pose for pictures. Shonke, it turned out, was a party chairman for George McGovern.

Still, like the fullback who keeps hitting the oversized line, these rebuffs have not dimmed Mr. Nixon's enthusiasm. He has sloughed them all off. During his first term, however, his love of sport involved him in two minicontroversies.

The first occurred in 1969, when the president attended the Texas-Arkansas football game. This was an end-of-the-season game between two undefeated, highly ranked teams. The president declared that the winner of the game would be the national champion. So, after Texas won, Nixon went down to talk to the team and to Coach Darrell Royal, and presented to the University of Texas (representing 26 electoral votes) a plaque for being number one.

The only trouble was that Pennsylvania State University, representing the great state of Pennsylvania (27 electoral votes), was also undefeated, highly ranked and truly believed it was number one. After President Nixon gave the plaque to Texas, the governor of Pennsylvania wired the White House, "What about Penn State?" Thousands of letters, telegrams and calls flooded the

White House. A handful of Penn State students and a German shepherd wearing a "Penn State No. 1" placard picketed the White House.

The White House became a bit ruffled by it all. Press Secretary Ron Ziegler tried to explain that the plaque given to Texas was intended only as a memento for the winner of that particular game during football's one-hundredth-anniversary year. It was pointed out to Ziegler, however, that the plaque *did* read, "To the number one college football team in college football's 100th year." That seemed to make that train of thought inoperative. Then, diplomatically, Ziegler announced that Nixon would present Penn State with a plaque of its own, this one to recognize Penn State's record of 21 consecutive victories, the nation's longest current winning streak.

But it was too late in the game for a sop like that. Pennsylvania's governor, Raymond Shafer, also a Republican, said, "We have no objection to this as long as they accompany it with another plaque designating Penn State as number one."

There were, naturally, various theories of how the president managed to embroil himself in this controversy. For instance, the southern-strategy theory: Texas and Arkansas both being southern states, Nixon was winning the South no matter which team won the game. Then there was the minority theory. This one has to do with Hugh Scott, senator from Pennsylvania and the Senate minority leader. Proponents of this theory believed that Nixon, unhappy with Scott because of the senator's defection on some key issues, wished to dump him. The plan was, allegedly, to infuriate Pennsylvanians with Nixon, and then for the president to campaign extensively for Scott when he came up for reelection. Thus, the voters, associating Scott with their football team's detractor, would vote for the opposition.

There were quite a few other theories, equally believable. Perhaps the most remarkable one is that the nation's number-one sports fan just isn't that knowledgeable and doesn't know a number-one football team from a bunch of plumbers.

Even though the controversy is over four years old, it still rankles some people at Penn State, like football coach Joe Paterno, who was the commencement speaker at the Penn State graduation in 1973. He spoke about football and he spoke about politics. "I'd like to know," said the coach, "how could the president know so little about Watergate in 1973 and so much about college football in 1969?"

The other minicontroversy over sports concerned the Dallas-Miami Super Bowl game of 1972. Normally in pro football, the president had explained, he is a fan of the Redskins. But after the Washington team was eliminated from the play-offs that year, he switched his allegiance to the Dolphins, the team closest to Key Biscayne. The Dolphins were the underdogs, so the president felt that the team needed some help. In a call to coach Shula, the president suggested a play: Send wide receiver Paul Warfield down and in against the Cowboys and throw to him. The Dolphins used the play in the game—and the pass was intercepted.

On the one hand, the Cowboys—and the Cowboy fans—were somewhat annoyed that the president—of all the people—should so flagrantly display his favoritism. And on the other hand, the Dolphins—and the Dolphin fans—were somewhat annoyed that the president would infringe on their territory.

The incident was not forgotten by either side. In 1971 the Dallas Bonehead Club presented the president of the United States with its illustrious "Bonehead trophy," which is presented "to the person or institution that has endeared themselves to the sports-minded public by their desire to participate and lose."

The next year, when Miami did win the Super Bowl, Don Shula, after thanking half the world for the victory, said, "I also want to thank the president for offering not to send in any more plays."

Nixon will probably not send in any more plays, but that surely doesn't mean he won't involve himself—publicly—with sports. Although he is the president, the most public man in the nation, Nixon is apparently a very private person. He finds it difficult to speak offhandedly, conversationally, with the masses. He prefers to sequester himself, to deal in memos, not people. Like the suburbanite who retreats at five o'clock from the tumult of the city to the privacy of his split-level, Nixon retreats to the private passion of sports. Although he must spend his time with kings and presidents, with princes of industry and academe, people with worldly interests, this is not his natural milieu. His avocational pursuits are not those of the upper classes but the those of the suburbanite, of the middle class.

After golfer Orville Moody won the U.S. Open title, the president called to offer his best wishes. Moody, a former air-force sergeant, recalled that "He congratulated me and said something about this not being a win for the elite but a big blow for the middle class."

Although sports *is* a private passion, it does give the private man an opportunity to go public. During the Cambodian invasion, and the subsequent protest, the president met early one morning with a group of protesters at the Lincoln Memorial. These were young people who were angry, who were appalled at the actions of their president and at the state of their country. The president asked the young people what schools they went to. When they told him, he immediately started to discuss their respective college football teams. The president naïvely thought he had discovered a common denominator to communicate with these people with whom he had very little else in common.

When the White House held a conference on drug abuse, to which they invited athletes from all sports, President Nixon went down the line of athletes and started each conversation with "I saw you on television..."

Sports is the president's method and his release. In his desk in the oval office, according to the Associated Press, the president keeps a real-life football. During some of the most difficult days of his presidency, the weekend when he fired Special Prosecutor Archibald Cox, when the attorney general and the deputy attorney general resigned, the weekend when the nation was in an anti-Nixon uproar, the president took time out to call George Allen, the coach of the Redskins. The president wanted to offer congratulations on the Redskins' 31–13 victory over the Saint Louis Cardinals.

"We just talked football," Allen later described the conversation. "We didn't talk about his problems."

Football, and other sports, have generally not been among Mr. Nixon's problems. It has been generally politically safe for the president to be a sports fan. The problems arise when Mr. Nixon starts to confuse sports and life. Like the time when he was speaking to the National Football Foundation: "I simply want to set the record straight with regard to my football qualifications," he told his audience. "This is a candid, open administration. We believe in telling the truth about football and everything."

WHO'S PLAIN?
WHAT'S AVERAGE?
10

The continuum runs from Richard Nixon to Alex and Bill. And the president is not alone at the top, because Bob Hope is there. So is Henry Kissinger. Barbra Streisand, too. Then there is Norman Mailer, Bing Crosby, Bill Cosby, Edmund Muskie, John Kennedy, Jr., Pearl Bailey, Neil Simon, Lorne Greene, Tiny Tim, the president of the Ford Motor Company, the vice-president of General Motors, Julie Newmar, Eugene Istomin, Budd Schulberg, Danny Kaye, Milton Berle, Justice William O. Douglas, former Chief Justice Earl Warren, Andy Williams, Dustin Hoffman, Elliott Gould, John Lindsay, Jack Kent Cooke, Joan Payson, Frank Sinatra, Robert Merrill, Spiro Agnew, Gerald Ford, and many others with unlisted phone numbers.

None of them are like Alex and Bill or Chris or Loudy. None of them sit, unnoticed, in the dank, unlit part of the stadium. None of them are plain, average, simple people who might need sports because their own lives are lacking in excitement. These are the movers and shakers of our world, the stars of stage, screen, finance and politics. They are also the stars of the arena. They are fans, too.

But they aren't fans the way most fans are. They are fans like stars should be fans.

They don't wait in lines overnight to make sure they get tickets. They don't have to fight their way through the crowd to get to the front of refreshment stands. When something exciting happens on the field, they don't have to tell the person in front of them to "sit down, ya bum."

There is usually no one in front of them.

Many of them are as fanatical in their devotion as the simple folk, but few of them create elaborate scrapbooks on their favorite players or collect autographed baseballs. It is somewhat difficult to imagine Henry Kissinger keeping a Billy Grabarkewitz scrapbook or Barbra Streisand asking Howard Twilley for an autograph. There are certain things that just aren't done, even in a democratic society. There is, after all, a difference in class involved here.

A few of this nation's aristocrats, however, do collect ball teams. It is one of the great advantages of being a fan and having a few dollars in your pocket. You buy a team to satisfy your fanaticism.

Many owners of sports teams will say that they made the purchase because it was a good investment, or they believed in the future of sport, or the future of the locality where the team is located. Sports is supposed to be big business, but compared to *true* big business, compared to General Motors and ITT, sports is little business. Very few professional sports franchises make money.

The reason many rich people buy teams is because they are fans, because the glamour and excitement of sports attracts them. They are intoxicated with the world of fun and games, and with its impact on the rest of the world. Phil Wrigley, the chewing-gum magnate, but more importantly the owner of the Chicago Cubs, once said he could put together the biggest business deals in the world and get only one paragraph in the *Wall Street Journal*, but when he fired Leo Durocher he made the front pages of every paper in the country.

Charles O. Finley is one of the biggest insurance men in the country. But no one heard of him until he started buying teams and putting sheep in the outfield. Jack Kent Cooke got more pleasure when his Los Angeles Lakers won a world championship than he ever did out of any of his Canadian radio stations. Andy Williams, Julie Newmar and Bobbie Gentry all like basketball, so they bought parts of a team. Dean Martin, Jackie Gleason, Glen Campbell, Bob Hope and Bing Crosby, all are fond of golf, and of golfers, so they've sponsored tournaments.

Sometimes the rich and famous, with all their money and glamour, simply never outgrew their more plebian passions. Ray Kroc, the McDonald's hamburger man and recent buyer of the San Diego Padres, tried to explain why he would spend so much money to get involved with such a financially and artistically disastrous proposition.

"I've been a stupid idiot fan of the Chicago Cubs since 1909 and I've been trying to buy them since 1965, and if you suffered with the Cubs for all those years you can take anything. And anyway, I just wanted a hobby. I'm in baseball so I can have fun."

Perhaps the most rabid fan from the moneyed classes has been Mrs. Joan Shipman Payson. Mrs. Payson is a Whitney, which makes her landed gentry. She is not new money but old and quite fashionable money. With her brother, Jock Whitney, she was heir to the immense Whitney fortune and owned Greentree Stables, one of the most prominent horse-racing organizations. But that was not her first love. Mrs. Payson's first love was baseball.

Her mother had been a fanatic New York Giants baseball fan, and so was Joan Payson. She loved the Giants so much that she bought stock in the company that owned the team. She developed a tremendous affection—in point of fact, a crush—for Willie Mays, the best of the Giants.

WHO'S PLAIN? WHAT'S AVERAGE? 133

Then, in 1957, the Giants, by vote of their stockholders, left New York. Joan Payson, a New Yorker, was desolated. She and her stockbroker, Donald Grant, were the only two stockholders who voted no.

Four years later, when the city of New York was desperately trying to obtain a new National League baseball team, the plotters went to Joan Payson. After a few meetings Mrs. Payson put up three million dollars for a new baseball team. It was, she said, a labor of love. "Whatever would not make me buy them?" she said. "Wouldn't anybody if they had the chance?"

Probably, Mrs. Dorothy Killam would have. Mrs. Killam, who owned paper mills throughout Canada, had never completely gotten over the National League's abandonment of New York. But unlike Mrs. Payson, she was a Dodger fan. Her devotion was pure, and expensive; she once spent $80,000 for an open telephone line so she could hear the full radio broadcast of the 1947 Yankee-Dodger World Series in Toronto, where she was recovering from an illness. When Mrs. Killam heard that the Dodgers were going to leave New York, she tried to buy the team, but was turned down. When a new opportunity came, with a new team, she joined the syndicate that owned the idea that was to become the Mets.

Mrs. Killam later dropped out, but Mrs. Payson is the only original member of the syndicate who stayed through the Mets' horrible early years, to be rewarded with the glory of a world championship. If the Mets were playing an important game and Joan Payson was in Greece, she would have the play-by-play given to her over the phone. Newspapers with box scores were sent to her in all parts of the world. Cost, of course, was not a factor.

Perhaps Mrs. Payson's greatest act as a fan,

money division, was her decision to bring Willie Mays over to her Mets. During the summer of 1972 the San Francisco Giants, in need of money, were looking to unload Mays. He had been their greatest player, their only link with a New York past, but he was finally quite obviously over the hill. The fastball was too fast for him now, and his legs didn't move with the grace or speed of the old days. But Mays's contract called for him to be paid in the neighborhood of $150,000 a year, an exorbitant sum for a team to pay for a ballplayer who was not really going to be of much use.

It wasn't a prohibitive amount for Joan Payson, though. Willie Mays had been her love, her idol, the object of her cheering. If she didn't have a Willie Mays scrapbook, maybe one of her servants kept one for her. Mays went to the Mets, and Joan Payson gave him a lush contract that would extend after his playing days were over.

Ah, to have money. To have money and be a fan. Even if you don't want to buy a team, money is quite useful in helping you indulge your passion. A lot of fans had a lot of money to spend for the 1974 Super Bowl. The game was held in Houston, near the center of oil country, and many of the oilionaires poured in for the big game. They didn't take the subway; they flew in on their private jets, like one great, expensive flock of geese. So many of them flew in, in fact, that the Houston airport couldn't take them all. The late arrivals had to land their planes at other airports, some of them almost 200 miles away. They didn't mind. There were always limousines to meet them.

But flying, if you have the money, isn't the only way to go. There's also the way Harvey Hester goes. Hester is a well-known restaurateur in Smyrna, Georgia, sort of a southern Toots Shor.

He is also a horse-racing fan, particularly a fan of the Kentucky Derby. He has missed just one Derby in over 20 years, and that one because he was sick. One year Hester decided he really wanted to *do* it, so he chartered an entire club car, complete with six sleeping rooms and a bar and a den. He invited six couples to go along with him. They lived out of that club car for three days. During the running of the Derby they sat in a glassed-in dining room atop Churchill Downs, situated about ten yards from over the finish line. The only difficulty with the whole trip, Hester said later, was that you had to walk too far to cash a winning ticket.

But perhaps the most sumptuous, the most extravagant, the most expensive and expansive fans are those of the Dallas Cowboys. Not all of them, of course. There are a lot of Cowboy fans who have to buy soy beans to make ground meat go a little further. But there are also Cowboy fans, and they are a tidy number, who know how to do this fan thing up big. This is the epicenter of oil country.

In Irving, Texas, just outside Dallas, the Cowboys have built themselves a little something called Texas Stadium, which is perhaps the most elaborate, efficient and highest-quality stadium in America. The top section of seats in the stadium, the most exclusive and most expensive section, is a series of private boxes the management calls "Circle Suites." This is a concept that was pioneered at the Astrodome in Houston. At the Astrodome, way up near the dome, all around, there are elaborate box-seat arrangements that aren't box seats at all. They are more like homes. They have their own bars and their own television sets and sometimes their own servants. The moving force behind the Astrodome, Judge Roy Hofheinz, naturally has the most elaborate box of all. What he has is a penthouse apartment, bedroom included, from where he can watch the game, or where he can sleep when not watching the game. Or he can go next door to the barbershop and get his hair cut.

Most of the Astrodome boxes were bought by corporations, so that the advertising manager could take the visiting vice-president to a game when the V.P. came to town. Visiting vice-presidents are fans, too. The concept has caught on. Madison Square Garden built hanging boxes from the roof of the building and leased each of them for $50,000 a year. Other arenas did the same. The boxes are for any event that takes place in the building, whether it is hockey, baseball, basketball or the regional play-offs for the punt, pass and kick competition. The locations generally aren't very good in any of the stadiums or arenas, but that isn't the important thing.

Status is important. You can take your box and make it into a second home. You always have a seat for everything, no matter if everyone else is shut out. Most importantly, you are removed from the masses, from the noisy, unkempt crowds that stand up in front when something happens. And if sports is now fashionable, as has been alleged, then this is the most fashionable way to indulge. If you want to keep up with the Joneses, it is no longer necessary to have three cars and two swimming pools. Have two bartenders in your private box.

The fans at Texas Stadium took the whole phenomenon one great Texas-stride further. They understood the real way to be real fans: real money.

They had to be true—and wealthy—fans just to buy a suite. There were 158 of them available to the general public and they didn't come cheap, which is why about half of them were bought by corporations. But the other half were bought by people, just good ol' fans. Each 16-by-16-foot suite cost $50,000 in stadium bonds. The 16-by-32-foot double suites went for $100,000. That was for the bare concrete box.

Then each suite owner was required to buy 12 tickets for each of the seven regular-season games and the two exhibition games, at $12 apiece. That's $1296 for the season, and the suite owner must buy those tickets for 32 of the next 35 years, during which his bonds come to maturity. If he does not buy the correct number of tickets, he forfeits his option to buy, the cruelest blow of all. The owner is allowed, however, to take one year off every ten years.

Then each owner must also buy a $25 membership for each seat in the exclusive Stadium Club. That's $300 a season. Then, of course, there's parking, for, say, six cars, at two bucks a shot for all the games—$108 per season.

So far the grand total is $51,704 for the suite, for only the first year of occupancy. And the suite is still just that bare 16-by-16 box. It cannot, of course, remain that way. It would be just a bit unprepossessing for a wealthy football freak to sit on the floor, unfed, untended. A little decorating is in order.

Most of the owners have spent at least $10,000 for the virtually mandatory comforts, which generally include a bar, refrigerator, automatic ice maker and closed-circuit TV set.

Moving on past the bare essentials, Toddie Lee Wynne, Jr., has an oak-paneled bar in his suite. Thomas Butler has a beamed ceiling and hanging kerosene lamps. W. C. Boedeker and Jack Burrell share an imitation zebra rug and South American sculpture. Frederic Wagner and J. L. Williams have blue velvet Louis XIV couches, gilt armchairs, blue velvet draperies, a minature bar with leather armrests, tufted velvet love seats, a crystal chandelier hanging from a vaulted gold ceiling, and hand-painted French panels concealing their closed-circuit television sets. The entire job cost $34,000.

But a football fan does not live on blue velvet draperies alone. So the Cowboy rich can order $20 trays of hors d'oeuvres, perhaps crabmeat claws or a shrimp bowl. If they prefer something a little more homey, they cook at home in their suites. One owner serves crepes from his microwave oven, while another is reported to serve pink papaya daiquiris.

The suites have become, just as the Cowboys advertised, "your 'personalized penthouse' at Texas Stadium . . . the ultimate in spectator luxury and comfort . . . similar to a second residence, like a lake home, or a ranch." The only way to go.

Actually, if you are rich and famous—particularly famous—you usually don't have to spend much at all to indulge your fanaticism. All stadiums and arenas make provisions for seats if the renowned should possibly request them. The promoters feel their product will shine with reflected glory if Henry Kissinger decides to attend their hockey game. So when Barbra Streisand, on the West Coast, decided at the last moment that she and her boy friend wanted to attend the second Muhammad Ali–Joe Frazier fight, on the East Coast, she put in a long-distance call to Madison Square Garden. This was a day or two before the fight, which had been sold out for weeks. But this was Barbra Streisand.

"I had two seats left," said Teddy Brenner, the president of the arena's boxing operation, "and I was saving them for my brother-in-law. Those were the two that went to Barbra Streisand. I couldn't turn her down."

When Frank Sinatra wanted to take pictures

of the first Ali-Frazier fight for *Life* magazine how was the magazine going to say no? When Bill Cosby wants to be on the sidelines at the Los Angeles Rams games, how can the Rams refuse? When Danny Kaye wants to sit in the broadcast booth at Dodger Stadium to watch his team, who would tell him that the booth was full?

When Bob Hope or Danny Thomas or Gene Autry want to buy into a ball club, who would not want to have them? Their money is good, but their image is even better. The stars give the teams visibility, and maybe even star quality. Whenever Bing Crosby's name is mentioned, there's always the chance that "Pittsburgh Pirates" will be mentioned too.

The glory, though, is reflected both ways. The stars get back almost as much as they give. They tend to be excited, fascinated, immensely respectful of athletics and athletes. The prominent actor, the famous comedian, the illustrious singer bask in the glory and the high fashion of sports. They may have been signing autographs all their lives, they have appeared during their careers before millions of people, but they are still in awe of men who throw and catch balls. Sports today is glamorous, fashionable, continually visible, and the dealers in glamour and fashion see that more clearly than most.

Performers also need to be physically fit and attractive, and maybe that's why they seem to have such an affinity for athletes. Maybe that's why so many theatrical celebrities have worked out with professional teams, frequently on an annual basis. The teams have been more than willing, knowing they weren't getting just another fan. So David Hartman, the actor, and the late actor Jeff Chandler used to work out with the San Francisco Giants. Charley Pride, the country-music singer, worked out with the Milwaukee

Brewers. Jerry Lewis used to work out with the Houston Astros. All of them have had considerable success in their fields but remain devoted to the remembrances of athletic promise past. "If I could've made it," said Charley Pride, who had a baseball tryout once, "I would've chosen baseball." Instead, he has had to content himself with workouts during spring training, and singing the national anthem at the last Super Bowl. It was as close as he could get.

"Actors and athletes have always had a great affinity for one another," explains Peter Cook, the British actor and comic and American sports fan, "actors, athletes and crooks. Criminals get along famously with people in our business. I think it is because they recognize in us fellow thieves. As entertainers, you see, we are also in the business of stealing the public's money. We are paid so disproportionately."

But not all celebrities are fans because of the glamour or even because they feel an affinity with ballplayers. Like Ray Kroc, and like most of us, the rich and famous probably were fans as kids. They also peered through knotholes. The rest of us grew up and stayed fans but were forced to continue to look through knotholes. But the rich and famous were able to get inside the fences. Rather than watching the ballplayers with binoculars, they are able to pose with them for photographs. The rich and famous may not have any more affinity for sports than the rest of us, but their affinity is much more visible and their desires are much more easily realized.

Milton Berle is one of those who never outgrew it. He has always been a sports fan, he says, and has always been involved in sports. He was an amateur boxer until the age of 16 when a knockout and a severe cut over his eye persuaded him to change his vocation. Even before he became Mr. Television, he was a boxing fan. There was the time, the comedian says, "I think it was 1945," when he went to spring training with the Giants. The team allowed him to hit once for Phil Weintraub. "So help me," Berle claims now, "I hit the ball out of the park. It's the truth, believe me." Only a very few do, but never mind.

Danny Kaye is another famous fan who used to be just a fan. He was a Dodger adherent when the team was still in Brooklyn. "We used to save our nickels to sit in the bleachers at Ebbets Field and rationalize that we had the best seats because we got the sun." Now he can sit with the broadcasters up in the radio booth. "But I would go to a ball game in Wichita and enjoy it," he claims. "What it adds up to is that I'm a baseball fan."

What it all adds up to is that you don't have to be rich, famous, influential, have contacts, move and shake the world to be a fan. But it doesn't hurt.

GIVING THEIR ALL: VIOLENCE AND THE FAN
11

Most of the mean people are now in the stands.
—Emlen Tunnell, pro football coach and former player.

In the early spring of 1955, the city of Montreal, Canada, the "Paris of the West," a sophisticated, cosmopolitan city, was convulsed by a riot. Thousands of Montrealers rumbled up and down St. Catherine Street, the city's major shopping avenue, breaking windows, looting stores, setting fire to automobiles. Tear-gas bombs were released——by both the police and the rioters. Fistfights were prevalent. Random stabbings and some shootings occurred. More than 40 people were eventually arrested. The riot was the most destructive one in modern Canadian history. Police estimated that over $100,000 worth of damage was done by the rioters.

It was a riot caused not by poverty, nor by animosity between different ethnic groups. It was not precipitated by an incident of police brutality, nor by an unpopular governmental decision. The rampage was set off by a city's love for a hockey team and a hockey player.

Al McGuire is a college basketball coach. Howard Cosell is a television and radio sports broadcaster. Reggie Jackson is a major-league baseball player. What they have in common is that in the last year each of them has been threatened with death.

Jackson was told he was going to be shot during the 1973 World Series. He had to have several FBI men shadow him during the seven games. A man in upstate New York wrote Cosell a letter saying he was going to "shut him up for good." After McGuire's Marquette team lost a close game to South Carolina, an irate woman fan called the Marquette switchboard and said she was so mad at McGuire she was thinking of shooting him. "I probably deserved to be shot the way I coached," McGuire said.

In 1972 Marv Hubbard, a fullback for the Oakland Raiders, returned from church on a Sunday to his hotel room in Kansas City to find a note shoved under the door. The writer of the note wished the fullback a good game, that game being "the last one you'll ever play on the planet Earth."

Hubbard has since minimized the note. "You should have seen the mail I got after the game was over," he says. "There was one sweet little girl who wrote to me and said that all she wanted from life was the chance to stand in line and spit on me. She even signed her name. What bothered me was the fact she expected to stand in line."

It was the third game of the 1973 championship series between the New York Mets and the Cincinnati Reds. In the fifth inning Cincinnati's Pete Rose and the Mets' Bud Harrelson got themselves tangled at second base and decided to fight. When Rose went out to left field in the bottom half of the inning, the fans pelted the outfielder with beer cans, cups, newspapers and one or two whiskey bottles. The Reds walked off the field. The president of the National League told the Mets they were in danger of forfeiting the game. Finally, the Mets sent out a delegation of players and the manager to plead with the fans to stop. After the game Sparky Anderson, the manager of the Reds, said, "It's awful dangerous to throw a whiskey bottle at a player. I can't believe that in this country today a man would do that. I'm not sure New York is in this country."

Former senator and minor-league ballplayer Eugene McCarthy was at the game and was asked whether he was worried about the violence. "No, not at all," he said. "Why should I be? Anyone who went through Chicago in Sixty-eight doesn't worry about anything."

The Austin, Texas, police department reported in 1973 a slight reduction in the toll of celebrants before the Texas-Oklahoma football game. The police said they arrested just slightly more than 200 people for various cases of fighting and assault. The year before it had been 278, police said.

Roy Spencer was a gravel spreader, living near Fort Saint James, in far northern British Columbia. His son Brian was a hockey player, and in December of 1970 Brian was called up to play for the Toronto Maple Leafs. Roy Spencer had propelled his son into professional sports and had been waiting all his life for this moment. His son was to be playing for his favorite team and Roy Spencer would be able to see the game. It was going to be televised on Saturday night, that week's selection for the "Hockey Night in Canada" series.

Roy Spencer sat down to watch the game. But instead of the Toronto Maple Leafs playing the Chicago Black Hawks, the game being televised was Vancouver against California. Roy Spencer, 59 years old and suffering from acute uremic poisoning, drove his car 80 miles through poor weather to the offices of the television station in Prince George, British Columbia.

Spencer stormed into the newsroom of the station, pulled a gun and ordered the station's news director to walk with him to the studio and

GIVING THEIR ALL: VIOLENCE AND THE FAN 145

take the Vancouver game off the air and put his son's game on.

One of the employees managed to call the police, and within five minutes they were there. Roy Spencer fired two or three shots, wounding one Royal Canadian Mounted Policeman in the leg, before he was shot in the chest and killed.

Among the artifacts thrown at athletes—and this is only in the last few years or so—careful research has discovered: beer, soft drinks, liquor bottles, other tyes of bottles, dead fish, live fish, rubber chickens, a fire extinguisher, knives, eggs (hardboiled and otherwise), bats, rubber balls, harder balls, a live rabbit, dead squirrels, firecrackers, rocks, pieces of apparel, newspapers, pens, pencils, seats, frankfurters (with and without the rolls) and assorted other bits of food.

Among the cities where a sports team winning or losing a championship has inspired riots or near-riots in recent years are: Detroit, Pittsburgh, Boston, New York, Miami, Washington.

Among the bars where the relative merits of the Dolphins versus the Raiders or of Mickey Mantle versus Willie Mays have provoked aggravated assaults are:—well, check the yellow pages, A to Z.

Sports fans and violence have seemingly always been entwined with one another. Fans are supposed to be spectators, passive veiwers, removed from the ferocity of the combat. But they are also urged to root, to form allegiances, to identify, to scream and shout and pray for the good guys. Somewhere along the line, the demarcation point gets blurred.

We are passive, a nation of sheep, but our games seem to bring the violence out. We are normal people, quiet people, reserved, definitely nonbelligerent. And then the game. "Honestly," says Hal Freeman, the president of Philadelphia's Spectrum arena, "I think if you brought fifteen hundred honor graduates of Episcopal Academy something might happen."

Whenever a new incident occurs, whether large-scale or two ten-year-olds throwing peanut shells, the editorial writers bemoan how the city, or the arena, or sports, or fans in general have had their reputations tarnished. Things are getting out of hand, it is written and said; these kind of destructive incidents didn't happen back in the good old days; what's happening to people in this crazy world?

Of course, they were saying and writing the same things back in 1934 when Detroit Tiger fans threw everything they could find at Saint Louis outfielder Ducky Medwick during the World Series. When the Montreal fans rioted in 1955 because their idol, Maurice Richard, had been suspended for the remainder of the season for fighting, the words were heard again. When there was an attempt in the late Sixties by losing bettors to incinerate Suffolk Downs in Boston, another uproar.

But perhaps things *have* changed slightly. It is, after all, a more violent world than it used to be. Or at least we are more aware of the violence around us. Throughout the Sixties, television brought the Vietnam War into our living rooms. We were forced to live with defoliations and search-and-destroy missions. When we turned away from television, Truman Capote was there to tell us the intimate details of a gruesome murder. Norman Mailer informed us about local armed confrontation. We kept tallies on the comparative totals of Richard Speck and Charles Whitman and Juan Corona. Our peaceful sanctuaries, the campus and the church, were invaded by police and the threat of imminent violence. Crime—meaning violence—in the streets has become the single most prominent social issue. The bars broke down and we were told to "let it all hang out." We did, and what hung out wasn't very pretty. Violence is all around us.

"I'm afraid violence is one of the entertainments of the mob today," says Clarence Campbell, the president of the National Hockey League. "If people could've bought tickets for the Vietnam War, they probably would've."

Bud Vye, the manager of Philadelphia's Veterans Coliseum, says, "Fans definitely are more aggressive now. And they drink more, too." A spokesman for the Atlanta Falcons says, "Fans definitely are more aggressive than when the Falcons started seven years ago." In Foxboro, Massachusetts, the manager of Schaefer Stadium says, "Abusive language, excessive drink, and violence seem to be a way of life now."

Fans are part of and reflect their violent world. The violence of sports fans cannot be dealt with in a vacuum. It cannot be packaged, compartmentalized, filed away. There are different varieties and varying reasons, and they are all very complex.

The kind of violence which seems to most offend the editorial writers is public, group violence. All the glib psychological catchphrases are dragged out here: "mob psychology," "exhibitionism," "group hysteria." And one police phrase: "crowd control."

This kind of violence, seen on the front pages and in the living rooms, creates an extremely difficult situation for team owners, managers and officials. If all this beer-throwing and fighting is going on in their stands, it appears that they are running a shabby operation. It looks like they should have put their money into hiring enough uniformed guards instead of into the new, exploding, contracting, living, breathing scoreboard.

But more importantly, the public violence forces the teams to make an ethical choice. Can they discourage beer-throwing and fighting when they've spent all this time and all this promotion money to encourage rabid fanaticism? They've urged their fans to become involved, to care, and what are they to do when the fans become a little too involved, or care too ardently?

When confronted with examples of public violence, the teams try, unsuccessfully, to tread water. A Pittsburgh Steelers official pleasantly acknowledges that "our football crowds do tend to get thoroughly involved." An official with Pinkerton's, Inc., the security people, says, "Fans are quite devout and they tend to get right involved emotionally."

When the New York Knicks beat the Baltimore Bullets in a play-off series in Madison Square Garden a few years back, Coach and General Manager Red Holzman claimed, "Our crowd beat their crowd." When fires were lit in the stands after a hockey play-off game, Madison Square Garden officials didn't comment.

The teams try to attribute the violence to "over-exuberance" or an excess of enthusiasm. Sometimes they say there was just a little too much drinking going on. But they're only looking at the tip of the iceberg.

It is generally assumed that the people who fight in the stands or throw bottles at the athletes do not do that kind of thing away from the stadium. (It is an assumption that has not been questioned, except when teams blame violence on "outside hoodlums," agitators, people who do that kind of thing in other places, but not our people.) If the assumption is even partially correct, then what happens to these nice people inside the arena? What is it that causes them to become violent inside the gates?

We live controlled lives. Walk. Don't Walk. Step to the end of the line. Quiet, please. We are continually told to control our natural impulses. Then, suddenly, we are in the arena and we can let loose.

"The fan, if he wishes, can express his emotions verbally and even physically without fear of censure," says Dr. Arnold R. Beisser. "It helps people to yell and release energy," says Dr. Milton Reisner. "But some have difficulty in controlling themselves once they let themselves go." In other words, once the gate has been opened, you don't know who or what's coming through.

When the gates are opened, thousands pour through. Over 100,000 people will get together to watch a college football game. More people can fit into Yankee Stadium or the Los Angeles Coliseum than there are people in some towns. Sports fans are almost always found in crowds. A crowd, of course, can be an apprentice mob.

"Basically, man is a flock animal," says Dr. Henry Kellerman. "He wants to be involved in something larger than himself so he can lose himself."

Anonymity. A sea of faces and bodies, and out from the middle of them comes a flying bottle of Jack Daniel's. It lands in front of Pete Rose, and Rose looks up to pick out the one who did it, and all he can see is a sea of faces and bodies. "The fan enjoys a peculiarly luxurious position between the camaraderie and the anonymity of the crowd," says Dr. Beisser. "He can have intense feelings, and act upon them with strangers who understand." Not everyone understands.

It was at the end of the second period in a hockey game between Saint Louis Blues and the hometown Philadelphia Flyers. Saint Louis coach

Al Arbour walked slowly toward the center of the ice to argue with the referee about a call that had gone against the Blues. Arbour followed the referee into the tunnel that leads to the official's dressing room. Just as the coach moved into the tunnel, from the stands directly overhead came a cup of beer, or maybe it was a soft drink. It poured all over the Saint Louis coach.

Ignition.

Immediately 14 of the Blues players charged across the ice and into the tunnel. Defenseman Bob Plager went over the railing and into the stands, wildly swinging his stick. Other players followed, swinging sticks and fists at the fans. Some fans fought back, while others hurled cups and other debris at the coach and players. Police swinging billy clubs eventually pushed the players out of the stands, and for a moment or two the world was calm. Then Plager, because of some affront or another, led a second charge into the stands. By the time all the furor had ceased, 150 police had been called, two policemen had been injured, two hockey players had been injured and four hockey players had been arrested. No injuries to fans were reported. No fans were arrested.

Hockey particularly seems to bring out the violence in fans. So does boxing. Football does, to a somewhat lesser degree. The reasons aren't buried in the psyches of individual fans, or in the psychoses of mass hysteria. The reasons are in the sports themselves. Both football and hockey have been served up as *the* sports for the modern era. Fast, explosive, violent, they are said to reflect the organized, tactically useful violence of today. Boxing has always been the underside of society, our baser instincts stripped of the civilized veneer we put on them. It is debatable whether these sports reflect our world. It is just as likely, perhaps more so, that our world reflects theirs.

The psychologists claim that violent sports are useful, giving us an outlet for the latent violence that is in all of us. A "safe release for aggressive drives," Dr. Reisner calls it. Sometimes, the release is not so safe. The jabbing and hooking of boxing, the full-team brawls of hockey, the forearm smashes and crack-back blocks of football give a justification for violence. The lines blur between stands and field. They are fighting down there and at worst are receiving five-minute misconduct penalties. More often, they are applauded, cheered, deified for their violent acts. Violence is good down there on the playing field.

"Of course," Dr. Reisner admits, "it's the behavior of the players that's tapping the fans' unconscious aggressive drives.

"In violent sports, like hockey and football, when the fans see blood they get interested. In baseball it's just the opposite. Everyone gives a gasp and they're very concerned about the safety of the players. When someone in authority kind of gives a go-ahead to violence, as they frequently do in hockey, there's a greater chance of mob hysteria. It's a form of encouragement. And once mob hysteria spreads to the audience, it's like Hitler addressing a mob and working it into a frenzy."

A little encouragement, which was Pete Rose throwing punches at Bud Harrelson, and even the calm baseball fans at Shea Stadium started throwing debris. Ducky Medwick didn't become a target until after he had fought with another player.

Sports like hockey and boxing also tend to incite violence because the fans are so close to the playing surfaces and the justifiable violence. "In hockey," says Clarence Campbell, the league president, "the fan is so close he is a participant.

If there's violence on the ice, he is naturally drawn into it."

But you don't have to be sitting rink- or ringside to be violent. You can sit anywhere. Football fans are not near the playing field, but that hasn't stopped them from engaging in homicidal acts. Baseball fans, too. In fact, you don't have to be anywhere near the ball park itself and it doesn't have to be anywhere near game time. The night before the Oakland-Pittsburgh football play-off game in 1972, Steeler fans stood in front of the Raiders' Pittsburgh hotel, shouting, overturning some cars, beating on the doors of the hotel. By the time two Raiders came out of the hotel, the situation was almost riotous, the players were pushed around and later had to receive medical attention.

These fans obviously were incited by stimuli other than the game itself. Maybe it's exhibitionism. Perhaps it's frustration. It could be sort of sports nationalism, or local chauvinism. There is also the ethnic factor, sometimes called race or religion or national background.

Twice in the Sixties a young Puerto Rican lightweight boxer named Frank Narvaez fought at Madison Square Garden. Narvaez had strong roots in the local Puerto Rican community. He was a symbol for it, a torchbearer. He lost each fight, by decisions that were quite close. After each decision, bottles rained down on the fight ring, chairs were ripped from the floor and thrown as far as they could be thrown, flaming newspapers—torches—were thrown for the honor of the torchbearer.

In Southern California, the last bastion of regularly scheduled professional fistfighting, the promoters have kept the pot boiling by appealing directly to ethnic pride. Jose Napoles, the welterweight champion of the world, a resident of

GIVING THEIR ALL: VIOLENCE AND THE FAN 153

Mexico, parades into the ring accompanied by men in sombreros carrying a billowing Mexican flag. Mexican songs are played. The opponent, from Santo Domingo, or Panama, wherever, gets similar accompaniment. Yes, occasionally they've had a little trouble in the fight palaces of Southern California.

Not all of the violence involving sports fans occurs in the sports palaces. Not all of it is triggered by mob hysteria and violence on the playing field. But those incidents are the ones that are most public and the ones that have been recorded.

No records are kept about how many times two men, friends perhaps, slugged it out over two teams or two players or one referee's call. There are no numbers telling of the times a husband casually brutalized his wife for interrupting a telecast of the game. How many times has someone had a couple of drinks, thought he was king, seen an athlete at the park bar and decided to challenge him? Who keeps records on how many times irate fans have written or called Howard Cosell, telling him they were going to shut him up for good?

We are urged to get involved, to care. It's the American way. And as Eldridge Cleaver has written, "Violence is as American as apple pie."

GIVING THEIR ALL: SEX AND THE FAN
12

She is called Detroit Shirley. She has sex with athletes.

It is the salient fact of her life. It is how she is defined, how she defines herself. The jobs she has had are unimportant. Her background is not relevant. Her plans for the future, her involvement in community activities, her relatives and her hobbies are not factors. Detroit Shirley is known and wants to be known as a sports fucker.

She is real. The name is Detroit Shirley, but she is not a character out of Damon Runyon. She is in her early thirties, is from Detroit and lives and works out of that city. She is five feet two inches tall, blonde, and although her face has a hard quality about it, her body is firm and supple. She calls it her "baby body."

She is not a prostitute; she does not do it for money. "I wouldn't accept it if I was offered money," she says in her small voice, "because that would be a form of blackmail. I wouldn't anyway. I never have. The only time I ever took any money was once or twice from the guy who ran the bar and he knew that I needed a couple of extra bucks and it was an incentive for me to come down. But I only did that a couple of times."

She does what she does because she is crazy for athletes, fanatical about them. They are the people she idolizes, cares most about. She enjoys sports, watches some games on the tube, but her involvement is much deeper. She is attracted to athletes, and to show her devotion she is willing to give the most precious thing she owns, her body. Rooting is not enough. Even throwing bottles is not enough. She is the ultimate fan.

She has been making it with athletes since she was 18 or 19, and now she is unable to say exactly how many athletes, how many times. But she can say, "I've seen all the American League baseball teams and more than half of the National League teams. In football, I covered all the good football teams, all the better football teams. Like I've seen the Redskins and I've seen the . . . let me see . . . the only ones I didn't see that were pretty good were the Dolphins. And I've seen most of the hockey teams.

"And every team that I saw I probably saw all of the team or at least half of the team. Many times I saw coaches and many times I even saw managers and things like that."

Shirley does not keep records of the comings and goings—as she says one of the girls who "does the same kind of things" does—but she says she doesn't need to. "I've got it all up here in my head," she says. "It's all mental. I know what I've done."

She is not bragging when she talks about it. It is said with a toneless little laugh and an air of quiet accomplishment. She is not bragging, but she is, she admits, a little proud. It's not the numbers, it's the quality, and to Shirley, ballplayers are quality.

"Listen," she says, "I just like men. But I like certain men in particular, too. And athletes are the most virile men around. Other men just can't compete with them. Other men just aren't superstars. I could go to bed with probably J. Paul Getty, but I can't see him on television playing baseball. And I can't read about him in the paper every day. Ballplayers are special. They're a special breed and they're a special type of people. They're just special. I don't know how else to say it. They have that supremacy . . . I don't know . . . because they are athletes. They're better sexually, at least baseball players are. That's my own personal survey there.

"You know, first I went for ballplayers because they're usually good-looking guys, they're clean and they're around my age. But I found out that they were different somehow. They're ego-trippers, and I like that. I guess that's because I'm on my own ego trip. I mean, I watch somebody on television and say I've been to bed with them. Sure. It sets me apart. It makes *me* a little better, I guess. I mean, they're famous people and I've been to bed with them and I know what they're like sexually, I know what they're like a little mentally and I know what they're like a little off the turf, I guess you could say. Sure it sets me apart."

Shirley is proud, but she is not blind. She exalts athletes as a class, but she can also be discriminating.

"Football players are lousy," she states with very little equivocation. "For one thing, baseball players like orgies and football players don't. Not that I'm an orgy person, but baseball players are just more sexually acclimated. They don't have the hang-ups that other people do. They can go with somebody, without somebody, with any kind of situation, they can cope with it sexually. Football players aren't that flexible.

"Now hockey players are okay," she says in a shoulder-shrugging voice, "but I think they've changed. To me, before, they were great screwers, now they're not. Now they just seem like . . . I don't know, hockey players are not as great as they used to be, to me. Now they're just kind of funny. I even had a very bad incident with one particular team where I had a thing where I was ready to sue them because I was so mad. I was really mad with the whole situation. It was a really bad situation. I can't even watch a hockey game anymore. I guess I have a definite dislike for hockey players now. But before they were generally nice.

"I mean there were some hockey players who were real nice, true gentlemen. And then I go meet another team and they're complete assholes."

Shirley is quite precise in her judgments. She is experienced and knows what she likes and what she doesn't. She takes it all very seriously. Her distinctions are not superficial.

"Right now," she says, "baseball players are my favorite. And baseball pitchers specifically. That's because they're built——they're my dimensions sexually and they're very physically attractive. The physical attraction is there because they're quite muscular, and the sexual thing is there because they're quite well endowed. I guess that's because they work out so much. You know, a lot of football players, like they don't work out too much and they're not in shape. They can't fool me. I know who they are."

They all know who Shirley is, too. And they know what she'll do for them. "Anything. I'll do anything. Way-out sex, things like that, anything. The only thing I wouldn't do, this baseball team wanted me to run out on the field, this one time, and drop my pants and this and that, you know, and get a lot of publicity for it because they were trying to make a pennant or something like that or they knew they were going to make the pennant. I said, well, I would think about it, but then that day I was supposed to do it it was too cold, you know, and I think that's the only reason I didn't do it. Otherwise I would've."

And they know where to find her. "There's this bar in the Detroit area that's frequented by baseball and football players," she says. "You know, that's how I started. I was going with this guy in advertising, I was about eighteen or nineteen, and we went to this place. It was a real sewer hole. Anyway, when I saw all the athletes there and I saw all the things that were going on in the bar, I liked it, so I went back and tried to make friends with them et cetera.

"The first ones for me were the football players because when I first went there it was the football season. This was my first acquaintance with athletes. When it was the next season, I got on to the baseball players, and like that.

"Anyway, if there's a certain team I want to get with, I make it a point to know the team's schedule. I find out when they're in town and I just go down to the bar. Everybody always comes in there and I'd be waiting for them. I just made it a point of knowing the schedule.

"Generally, that was where they could find me. Sometimes, if there's a team I really want to see and they're in another league or something, I'll travel out to meet them and things like that. But I won't really travel *with* any of the teams. I don't go in for that much."

Shirley has, by her own account, "been fucking around with the athletes" for about eight or nine years total. She stopped when she was about 25 and then after two years away went back for a year or two. Now she has stopped again. She stopped because "I don't want my face all, you know, smashed around." She will miss it, she says, because "some guys I met I would gladly pay and I never said that in my life."

But the ballplayers won't miss her. They might not even know she's gone, there are that many other bodies around. "Many other girls are doing it now," Shirley claims, "more so nowadays than ever before. I guess that's because of the pill and things of this nature. And because the heroes that you have to look up to—I mean the ballplayers, they're looked up to more as heroes now."

The heroes used to be all around us. The movies offered up Clark Gable and Gary Cooper and Errol Flynn. From the battlefields came Douglas MacArthur and Audie Murphy. Before Dallas and the Ambassador Hotel, even politics seemed to be peopled with heroic figures.

But this is an antiheroic time. Clark Gable and Gary Cooper have been replaced by Dustin Hoffman and Al Pacino. They may be fine actors, appealing and cuddly, but they do not inspire images of heroism, or sexual fantasies. In a world of My Lais, soldiers are suspected of moral treason. Politicians are no longer representative of our ideals, our heroism, but of our shame.

It was not so much that Gable, MacArthur and Kennedy were good-looking, although that was part of it. They had flair, performed distinctively. They made us feel they were capable of anything. They could stretch themselves to the limit, and so they were able to stretch our imaginations.

There are almost no heroes like that left, no supermen left on whom to hang our fantasies, our wet dreams. But the need for heroes has not abated. We still want to believe that there are people who can stretch reality, who can scale heights the rest of us only dream of. We look for characters who can take us out of the routine, lift us from our mediocrity. The classic heroes may be gone, but we try to make do. We find our heroes where we can.

The microboppers and the teenyboppers have chosen rock musicians as their spokesmen, their ideal. Wherever the rock stars go, they are trailed by their groupies, their plastercasters, pubescent idolators wobbling on three-inch platforms. The rest of us, less musically inclined or youth-oriented, have chosen athletes. They have become our sexual totems.

It is the athlete as superstud, the athlete as sexual ideal. They are young and physical, engaged in great combat and daring. They are attractive, but also vulnerable, which seems to make them even more attractive. They are usually larger than the rest of us, and on the field they seem larger still. Their stages stretch from coast to coast, and their performances go on through all seasons. They are our Clark Gables.

They know it, too. Joe Namath, with a wink and a leer, tells you he's about to get creamed or pushes his new line of bed sheets. Walt Frazier describes in intimate detail for the woman's-page writers the mirror above his bed. Wilt Chamberlain, in his autobiography, smugly reveals that he has known upwards of 3000 women.

They revel in it. It is confirmation for them of their exalted status. "The chicks, they're everywhere," says Billy Paultz of the New York Nets. "And the guys think they're really hot stuff with the chicks hanging all over them." As Detroit Shirley says, it is an ego trip for them. They can pick and choose, stay a long time or just stay the night. They can have it any way they want it. They compare notes on their women, sometimes exchanging names, places, even bodies. It is a comfortable world for them. They know the women are there, just waiting. The baseball players call them "baseball Annies," the football players have their own nicknames, and all the athletes know where to look. The women are waiting by the clubhouse door or near the bus in the parking lot. In each city there are bars that the athletes always go to, and the girls know which ones. They are there, by the bar, talking to the man making the drinks and figuring out when the last inning or final quarter will be ending.

Sometimes they will not be in their accustomed places. Sometimes, if the players are pleased, a girl might travel with a team. "There was this girl, during the play-offs a year or two ago," says an official of an NBA team. "I can't remember her name, but the players had a nickname for her. Everywhere I went, I saw her. She was near the clubhouse in all the cities we went to, near all the different buses we had, everywhere. I guess one of the guys was giving her money to come around."

Sometimes the players don't have to go anywhere at all. The girls come to them through the post office. It is the ultimate fan mail.

They will get letters offering to cook them meals, to help get them out of their slumps. There will be suggestions on how they can take their minds off the game. Tommie Agee, the baseball player last with the Los Angeles Dodgers, once received a typical letter: "Dear Tommie," the lady wrote, "I am 22, very good looking, have a nice figure, am not conceited and all the boys like me. I'll kill myself if I don't meet you. My address is——— My phone number is———"

The volume of mail is enormous, particularly for the star. "I get an awful lot of letters from girls, and it varies what they say," says Jim Plunkett, the star quarterback. "A lot of them start out with 'You probably think I'm crazy for writing this letter. But I saw you in a game on TV [or I saw you at the home game] and I'd like to tell you a little about myself.' You know. Then they say they're five feet four, a hundred and twenty pounds, blonde hair, blue eyes. Sometimes they send a photo. As a rule, most of the time, they're really nice-looking."

Derek Sanderson, the hockey player, was the prize in a contest held a few years ago called

"A Date With Derek." The letters poured in, and with them came thousands of photographs, many of them nudes. The winner, without a nude photograph, was a grandmotherly grandmother.

The women, whether by post or in person, are as varied as the letters. There are the teen-age groupies, acned and baby-fatted, who want an autograph and maybe something more physical to tell their friends about. There are the housewives, bored with their homes, their husbands, their lives, who want a little more excitement than they have been allotted. The athlete is someone who can make them feel better than they've been told they are. He might show them something new. The athlete is a tunnel to the outside world.

There are the women, divorcées perhaps, in their forties and fifties, hard-faced women, who hang around the bars, smoking their cigarettes, chain-drinking their martinis. For them, making it with an athlete means they are still young, attractive, still relevant in a world of youth cult.

With the younger ones particularly, it is a close-knit society. Like other fans comparing decals and scrapbooks, they compare the athletes they've had. They might spread the word about who's around, who's available. "It's like a jungle telegraph," says the NBA official. "A new guy can come into the league, never seen the town before, and there's a girl waiting for him. I mean, they're not organized like hookers. They're not hookers. They're free samplers."

The players are more than willing to accept the free samples. But they have become somewhat careful in their choices of which free samples to accept, because their relationships with their ultimate fans have occasionally caused them trouble.

Back home, away from the stadium and the

dimly lit bar, there is usually a split-level and a wife, or at least a girl friend. "Most of the time," says Jim Plunkett, speaking generically, "the wives and the girl friends understand when a girl will send you a letter or come on with you in a restaurant. But they get upset, too. That's only natural. But I guess the reason they generally understand is because they know that in some sense you're public property and women think you're always available."

Sometimes the woman at home isn't that understanding. It took Mrs. Billy Rogell 40 years to lose her capacity to understand. After being married for 45 years to the Detroit Tigers star shortstop of the Thirties, Mrs. Rogel was granted a no-fault divorce in 1974. She testified at the hearing that Rogell, now 69, had been seeing a "woman fan" ever since he gave her an autograph in 1934. Billy Rogell said the fan was only a friend.

Sometimes the trouble is with the team. All teams know that their players occasionally philander, particularly on the road. Some teams have hired spies or given money to an assistant trainer or coach to report on the players' after-hours lives. But the teams generally tolerate the fooling around, mainly because they have no choice. They can't stop it. Another good reason is that sometimes the officials themselves are also involved. Most importantly, sports is a quintessentially man's world, a world where women are supposed to give pleasure. Sex is natural, and desirable, an outlet for highly physical performers. Fidelity is not an issue.

But the management doesn't wish to be blatantly confronted by it. They don't want to be embarrassed publicly and they don't want the team to receive bad press. So the players are made aware of certain rules of discretion, the major one being: Don't get caught. As Casey Stengel used to say, "I don't care where my ballplayers drink, but they don't drink in the hotel bar. That's where I drink."

Occasionally, management and athlete collide and there is an embarrassing moment. "It's two or three in the morning," says the NBA official, "and I meet one of the players and he's with a girl, taking her up to his room. 'This is my cousin,' he says. Well, I'll tell you, we got the biggest families in the world on this team. You know, I've never had a player who was an only child."

Sometimes the trouble is more than just a fleetingly awkward moment. Eddie Waitkus, a major-league baseball player some 25 years ago, was invited by a woman fan up to her room. Like almost every other athlete, Waitkus was glad to go. When he got there, she shot him.

Since then, athletes have generally been a little more careful about their liaisons. That doesn't mean they've said no any more than they used to. It's just too difficult. There are too many out there, too many for whom the athlete is the top of the sexual heap. They are the public, and the athlete is public property. They are the fans, the customers, and the athlete knows that the customer is always right.

Her name was Ellie, She was 14, maybe 15 years old. She was plump, unwrinkled, like a virgin pear. Had she lost 30 or 40 pounds she would have been pretty. But now there was something unfinished about her, as if she was wrapped in a fleshy cocoon and would eventually emerge as a dainty little butterfly. She had long blonde hair that cascaded over her shoulders and almost down to her bright green pants. She wore horn rims.

She was sitting on the steps, her legs angled out straight from beneath her. She was waiting in the

GIVING THEIR ALL: SEX AND THE FAN 165

gray and yellow corridor of Boston Garden, a dark and grim place. The floors were slick as ballboys scurried from one end to the other carrying trays of ice. It was two hours or so before game time and Ellie was waiting by the staircase next to the Boston Celtics dressing room.

Clanking down the corridor came two of Ellie's friends, from high school, she said. They whispered conspiratorially with each other, until a tall, elegant black man, a professional basketball player, walked by them. They stopped talking and waved. The basketball player gave a tightly bent forearm wave back.

"Hey," Ellie said to her friends, "you know who that is?" She mentioned the name of a fringe ballplayer, a player whose face and even name is unknown to most fans. "He just hurt his leg. Hurt it in Philadelphia. He was telling me about it." She told her girl friends that he had talked to her and was going to ask her out.

THE NATIVES ARE RESTLESS

13

It all began in the Sixties. The masses were taking to the streets, to the campuses—my God, even to the stock exchange. The passivity of the Eisenhower years was over. Every group was becoming a movement, demanding its piece of the cake.

It all began with the blacks. They wanted their rights. Then the students demanded *their* rights. Then the Chicanos said they were good and fed up and told everyone what they wanted. As the movements moved into a new decade, the women took their turn. Liberation was what they wanted. The homosexuals followed, demanding, on behalf of all consenting adults, the right to consent to anything. All the groups railed against the "establishment," a term which came to mean all the people who weren't in your group. There weren't many groups left to rail. Then, finally, the ethnics started picking up the cudgels. They were the beloved "silent majority," who, it seems, had been oppressed by the noisy minorities. At any rate, when they joined in, it seemed everybody was manning the signposts, loudly proclaiming their rights, vowing not to take anything sitting down anymore.

The only problem was, with everybody out there on the ramparts, with all that hyperactivity, all the energy seemed to drain out of the protest movement. The masses were exhausted. The students went back to studying and important political activities like running around without clothes on. The women devoted their time to consciousness-raising groups. The blacks went off to electoral politics and self-help activities. The

THE NATIVES ARE RESTLESS 167

homosexuals decided to neither switch nor fight. The streets became quiet. Was there no group left to pick up the banner of protest?

Yes, one group was left, a group that had become used to taking things sitting down. The last unsilent majority was getting ready to hit the sidewalks. The fans of the world are uniting.

Perhaps not exactly uniting. Perhaps not even throughout the whole world. But there have been rumblings.

In 1972, in Philadelphia, four Eagle football fans sued the club for being "inept, amateurish in effort, and falling below the level of professional football competence expected of a National Football League team." The four fans charged breach of contract and demanded that the Eagles refund the money they had paid for tickets to the remaining games during the season.

In Saint Louis an equally disgruntled football fan offered, in an advertisement, "a playbook illustrating all FIVE of the Cardinals offensive plays, including the squib punt."

During the 1972 National Hockey League season, hockey fans around Burlington, Vermont, bombarded Canadian Prime Minister Trudeau and the Canadian Parliament with telegrams and letters. The reason was that a local Burlington television station had been televising Boston Bruins hockey games, but the Montreal Canadiens had insisted that the telecasts be halted because they impinged on Canadien territory. A court suit was threatened. Meanwhile, a fugitive from Canadian justice was captured in Burlington, and the town was threatening not to return him.

In Buffalo, football fans sued—and won— over the right not to have to buy tickets to exhibition games if they wanted regular season tickets. Other groups throughout the country are starting similar actions.

The most effective tactic the fans have at their disposal is, naturally, not going to the games. When the Milwaukee Braves played their last season in Milwaukee as a lame duck, after they had announced they would be moving to Atlanta, the fans just stayed away. It wasn't that they liked the Braves or baseball any less. It was a matter of principle. And the fans, in their resolve, drew strength from each other. Perhaps if the Braves had had a good team that year and some fans had started to go, then others would have followed. But in unity there was strength.

That was the concept that Dominic Piledggi was banking on. Dom Piledggi, once a high-school biology teacher, presently a high-school vice-principal, was the founder, moving force and first and only president of Sports Fans of America. The movement of the movements had reached the noisy majority.

Dom Piledggi, of Catonsville, Maryland, is a moral man. "Dealing with kids, being an educator, I have to be a very moral kind of person. This is very important to me." Dom Piledggi is—actually, was—a fan, a man who went to all Baltimore Colt home games for seven years. He also went to a large number of professional baseball, professional basketball and professional hockey games each year. He goes to at least a couple of high-school basketball or football games a week. In the late Sixties Dom Piledggi's moral outrage and his devotion to sports coalesced. The result was Sports Fans of America.

"I got involved in this because of a moral issue," Piledggi starts the story. "I didn't get into it just so I could get better frankfurters or that parking facilities would be improved. I just got tired of people writing books and bragging about their life in bed the night before they go out and play football. I was tired of athletes who were stars and thought they got special treatment and owed no responsibility to the people who pay the freight. I got tired of management who didn't think they owed anything to the people who allowed them to operate. Everybody had an organization, had some kind of protection. All the players had their players associations. The owners were protected through their commissioners and their corporate operations. The only people who hadn't formed a group for their own protection were the fans, the most important group of all. I thought the fans needed to be protected."

Piledggi is the classic case of the hard-working, respectable, middle-class citizen who has just had it up to here. He's had it up to here with everybody else getting everything, and getting it at his expense. Dom Piledggi reacted to all the unrest of the Sixties. He became the backlash to the frontlash of the new liberated world. He had lived his life quietly, competently, meaningfully. He had done his job well, done what he had been told, listened, kept within the bounds of what was accepted, what was traditional. Meanwhile, everyone else was going outside those bounds. As a moral man, Piledggi was bothered. But he was not a joiner, not a movement type of person. Actually, he didn't really fit into any group. Well, he was a fan. And if he was outraged, he thought, so were a lot of others. If he was middle-class, he knew that almost all fans were middle-class, too. "I knew that most fans had to be upset when they read about or heard about some athlete making a hundred thousand dollars who was having difficulty making ends meet. And crying about it, too. You're a fan and you have to listen to that while you're making between six thousand and ten thousand a year.

I'd like to see one of those guys with their hundred thousand trying to raise a family on six thousand a year."

The main question was, even if the fans could all be brought together by class, what else could bring them together? Could they find a common cause? Just because the farmer in Iowa and the policeman in New Hampshire both made less than $50,000 a year and both liked hockey and basketball, did that mean they could join together in a movement?

"That's true," Piledggi says. "But to find a common bond, fans don't have to be similar in all ways. I thought that if we could all look at one aspect of the sports fan, that we all have to pay for tickets, if we all saw that as our common bond, then we could do something."

In a sense, Piledggi is one of the last of the true democrats. Equality for everyone. We are all in this thing together. The true democracy is the one where we all pay the price, even if it is only for tickets. "I was involved in the Little League," Piledggi says to illustrate his argument, "and you'd be surprised how many kids feel that 'I'm a star, I get special treatment.'"

For Piledggi, no special treatment, not even if you give it to yourself. "I became disgruntled with what I considered to be the selfish attitude of both players and management, the total disregard for people who pay the freight for sports —namely, the fan. I don't like to see people taken advantage of. I guess that really says why I started Sports Fans of America."

With a friend, Angelo Coniglio, Piledggi began the organization. Piledggi did most of the work. He contacted a computer company to do the mailing for the organization. He got on television, doing the "Today Show." He did a radio show with Joe Garagiola for a month. He even designed the emblem for Sports Fans of America. It's a picture of a man with his hands outstretched. He is in chains. Half of him is blue and the other half is white. There's a star over the left hand, a star over the right hand and a star over the head. "The thing that I was depicting is that the man was being torn in half," Piledggi explains pridefully. "The players were doing it on one end and owners and management on the other. While the true star of sports is on top of the fan, because to play before an empty stadium with no noise, well, that's not sports."

With their emblem hoisted high, and with 5000 members from 50 states (at four dollars a shot), Sports Fans of America embarked on its crusade. With Piledggi at the helm, it had some specific goals.

"I thought there were a lot of services the organization could render sports fans. Things like insurance, health plans, things like that. We had a lot of gimmicks like that in mind. If things had been successful, we would have had a commissioner of sports who would be paid for by sports fans. Through him, we would have power in a lobbying capacity and also on a negotiating basis. We wanted to be able to dictate to owners and management, just like the players do. We wanted to tell them, give the fan a voice. We wanted to tell the management and the owners what the fans want. Eventually, if we had gotten enough people behind us, we would've had the leverage for economic boycotts. I think economic boycotts are wonderful, and I think we'd have been in a position to use them. Obviously, that's the only way professional sports might have listened to us.

"Another one of our goals was to see the income-tax statements of every franchise owner in every professional sport. The idea was to see to what degree the federal government subsidized rich people's hobbies. Namely, are the Baltimore Orioles, for example, a separate entity, or are they part of the Hoffberger Corporation, where any losses are merely channeled into the National Brewing Company? Or how about the Wrigley chewing-gum people, who own the Cubs? Or CBS, which owned the Yankees? Not many people realize that football players are amortized over a number of years, for example. It would be very important to find out about that kind of thing, because I think fans are getting very tired of hearing about how much money a team is losing and so the costs of seats are going up, while in reality it's just a paper loss."

Like an idea whose time had not yet fully come, Sports Fans of America ran into problems. Perhaps the worst of them was the reaction of most people. People generally reacted to a movement of sports fans the way they would to a union of sword swallowers. If you don't like it, why do it? If you don't like the way you're treated at a game, why go?

"Yeah, we got that a lot," Piledggi remembers. "And it's true in a sense. In fact, that has been the logic behind the way sports has treated the fan. For too long their attitude has been 'You want to see major-league baseball, then you see it here or you don't see it.' So people would tell us, 'Okay, if you're unhappy, don't go to see it.' But we would tell them there is a difference. Here's an analogy. If I want to go out and buy an automobile, and I want to buy a Chrysler, I have a number of dealers from which to choose. If you're a fan, you have no choice. So even if you don't like the way things are run, what can you do about it? The owners think you can't do anything. But thinking like that is eventually going to kill the goose that lays the golden eggs."

There were other problems. Publicity was part

of it. "First of all," Piledggi details, "the publicity we got was mostly local. Sure, we got on the "Today Show," but who's watching TV at seven fifty-five in the morning? And the worst thing of all was that most of the publicity treated us as some kind of a joke. As a result, people figured it was just a gimmick."

Some time in 1971 Sports Fans of America ceased to exist officially. It died "because we were not able to recruit sufficient active members to make it pay its way." Informally, it still exists. "What that means," says Piledggi, "is that the records are still intact and a lot of the people who were involved in it are still in contact with each other. And the Congressional Committee that was investigating sports has our records and is going to be using them for a survey they'll be doing."

It lasted for only a couple of years, but Piledggi, still very serious, thinks Sports Fans of America did accomplish some things. "I think it accomplished a great deal, including my being asked to testify at the Senate hearings. That was the first time in the history of sports that a sports fan got to testify. It was the first time that someone could speak from experience about what it's like to go to games."

Piledggi accomplished that. What he also accomplished was to personally end his involvement as a fan, at least what he defines as a fan. "A fan," he says, "is an individual who on a fairly regular basis pays for a ticket out of his own pocket to attend a sports event. I'm not that anymore. I haven't seen a live football game in three years. I haven't seen a live baseball game in two years. I've become a living-room fan, and that's not really a fan, because the living-room fan doesn't actively support the team. A living-room fan contributes very little to the sport. He only takes from it. As a fan, I've become a parasite."

Piledggi says that because of his involvement with Sports Fans of America he has become "disenchanted, disillusioned." Like the revolutionary student who fails at creating a new order and moves from protest to eastern mysticism, Piledggi has become alienated. And so the banner was passed. Righteous movements never die, but the leaders change. The spark was still there. In Tucson, Arizona, a sports-fans union started up. An organization calling itself the National Association of Sports Fans rented office space in New York. The group said its purpose was to improve "fans' involvement and participation in decision processes affecting their well-being." In Boston, Eddie Andelman, who describes himself as "just a fan," hosts a radio show called "Sports Huddle," which seeks to be the "voice of the fan." Andelman has written a book called *Sports Fans of the World, Unite*. In California a group called The Fans League has been formed. In Minneapolis a man named Rick Pearson is trying to start a group called—maybe—Fans, Incorporated.

Rick Pearson is 27 years old, once a newspaperman, presently the publicity director for World Team Tennis. In sports Rick Pearson is an inside man. Dom Piledggi, like Mark Rudd and Stokely Carmichael and Ti-Grace Atkinson before him, learned that storming the fort from the outside is beating your head against the wall. Rick Pearson is inside the wall. His approach reflects it. He is more reasoned, more understanding. The chip on his shoulder is a little smaller.

And yet, the bulb that lit in Rick Pearson's head is not very much different from the one that went off in Dom Piledggi's brain. "It was Valentine's Day, 1973," Pearson remembers, "and I was watching television. They had this film clip on, asking the Minnesota manager Frank Quilici what he thought of the Players Association. I looked at my wife and I said, 'You know, everybody's got an association but the fan.' And that's when little things started going off in my head and I started thinking about computer ballots for all-star games and things like that. It just struck me that there were a lot of things that people would like to voice their opinion on, from relatively unimportant things like who gets the Heisman Trophy, to the quality of concessions in the ball parks, high prices, things like that."

Pearson understands that for fans to form a group, for them to find common cause, the bond must be much broader than just disenchantment with all-meat frankfurters that are 30 percent chicken. For all fans to join together, the full gamut of fan interests must be dealt with. Unlike Piledggi, Pearson believes that a fan isn't just the "individual who on a fairly regular basis pays for a ticket out of his own pocket to attend a sports event." With analytical flair, Pearson can dissect what went wrong with Sports Fans of America. "If you try to make it a big damn deal, a lot of people don't like it. Everybody who's done it seems to have gone into it with a chip on their shoulder. What I want to do is start it out with something fun to do, so that you could involve yourself in something enjoyable. It'd be something you could vote on, like you'd have a computer punch-out ballot with the top ten or fifteen college football players. You'd have your own Heisman Trophy ballot."

In public-relations terms, it is called "the hook." Get the people interested. Then, Pearson feels, you could follow the route of Dom Piledggi. "Eventually you'd intend it to go the way the guy in Maryland wanted it to go. Eventually it could become a lobbying force. I'd want it to get to the point where we had our own attorney, our own Marvin Miller. And like Marvin Miller does for the baseball players association, our lawyer would do for us.

"Let's hypothesize. Suppose you have a quarter of a million members, and you have this lawyer. We poll our quarter of a million and we get an overwhelming mandate from our fans that they would like to see the National League adopt the designated-hitter rule. Our lawyer takes this information, takes the computer breakdowns, to the National League president. The lawyer points out that this survey indicates that the fans like the rule. And the National League president says, 'I don't care.' So the lawyer takes the survey with him and calls a newspaper columnist in San Francisco, and one in New York, and one in Detroit. And he tells them, 'Guess what, the National League president says he doesn't care what a quarter of a million fans think.' Then he presents the stats to the writer and tells him this is what the fans said. I can't really fantasize that every time the National League owners have a meeting they're going to ask somebody from our organization to come up and join in it. But after you do something like this, you know they're going to listen."

The whole key to Pearson's approach, in the classic public-relations tradition, is the media. "When I say we're inside," Pearson explains, "what I mean is we know how to use the media. I know people at the wire services, at the *Sporting News*, places like that. I know how to get things in the papers and on television. What the other people who have tried to organize something like this don't understand is that you have to get attention for this. Publicity is essential. Like, we'd do it with our version of the Heisman Trophy. When our vote comes in we get a mug shot of the winner moved on the wires. People then know who you are. When you deal with a National League president, that gives you some believability. You have to have that, you have to show some kind of results, to keep the membership interested. The whole key to the thing is to keep people renewing their annual fee. Apparently, that's what the other groups have failed to do."

Pearson envisions a large, expensive (five dollars a head), complex and ambitious organization. You can't run it out of your garage, he says. "The things I have in my head probably would cost a lot of money per member. But if you had enough members, you'd have a substantial budget, and then you could really do things. I'd like to use something like the Stanford Research Institute, and professional survey writers, so you could take all the things apart. You could find out who voted for what, where. Eventually you could start a monthly magazine that would bring up issues that affect the membership. From there, I think, you could get into maybe endorsements, like for those tabletop games. There are a lot of marketing aspects."

The plans are grandiose, but so far they are just plans. Pearson hasn't done anything with them yet. The organization doesn't exist yet. "Outside of putting things down on paper and talking to people about it, we've done very little with it," he concedes.

There are problems delaying the project. "The main problem is to do it right, and that's really the only way to do it. You need some pretty good funding going in. That's because there are some absolutes. For instance, you would have to have an ad with a membership blank at least once a month in *Sports Illustrated*, the *Sporting News*, *Sport* magazine, all the magazine annuals, the big newspaper sports sections. Now that's a lot of money and that's why we haven't started yet. What we have to do is to find some people to sort of endow it. The question is, what kind of people would do that? I mean, there's some great sportsmen around, like Tom Yawkey in Boston, but it can't be anybody who's an owner. Neither can it be one of the players associations. And it can't be anybody who wants to use the organization for his own purposes. It really has to be somebody who just likes sports and has about a hundred thousand dollars to throw around for an endowment fund. That's for the first year. Somebody to underwrite it for the first year, that's all you'd need."

So far, no one has come forward and offered Pearson the money. That doesn't mean, he hopes, that nobody will. "It's going to be difficult, but not impossible. I really want to do it. I talked to a friend of mine about it, a guy who's an agent for some of the big names in sports, and he told me it's a brilliant idea, and it's only a brilliant idea because the guy that got the idea is the guy that could pull it off. We could pull it off, we really could."

Meanwhile, Pearson will wait, with his marketing gimmicks and computer plans and "very practical approach," until his money man comes along. He'll continue to wait because, after all, his motivation isn't that different from Dom Piledggi's. "I get pissed off a lot, if that's what you mean. Yeah, I get irritated about the way fans are treated. I don't really care who's right anymore, the owners or the players. I just think the fans are getting the short end of the stick. I think, for instance, that national rankings are a crock. I don't like having to buy preseason games as part of the season-ticket plan. I think the football-blackout thing is probably wrong. I get livid sometimes about the Olympics and the silly stuff that goes on there. I mean, Coca-Cola being the official drink of the games. What really bugs me is something like one league having a rule like the designated hitter and the other league not having it. That's ridiculous. And I don't like paying sixty cents for a bottle of 3.2 beer at a football game. That's a joke. You're damn right I'm pissed off."

Whether they are on the East Coast or in the Midwest, whether they carry a chip on their shoulder or a print-out in their hand, the natives are getting restless.

Do you know where your little sports fans are tonight?

OVER THERE
14

We are a provincial people. Our vision is tunneled, beginning and ending at the Atlantic and Pacific. We see ourselves as the focus, the sun around which the rest of the world revolves. We think everyone speaks English and wears suits.

We call our best teams "world" champions and can't conceive of others doing things differently, or better, or doing things we have not even heard of.

We think the world of sports turns on Joe Namath and Johnny Bench and can't identify the name Pelé. When we talk of sports, we talk of baseball and football. We can't imagine that the most popular game in the world is soccer. We even call it by its wrong name. It's not soccer, it's football. But to us, football is Larry Csonka.

We can't imagine that people could care so much about a sport where you can't use your hands. We think being a fan means buying a season ticket or making a banner out of an old bed sheet. We don't know that over there it is a little bit different.

Sports fans in other countries do have many things in common with sports fans here. They don't like their teams to lose. They are rabid. They show their fanaticism in many different ways. But, still, they are very different over there.

It is difficult, of course, to generalize about "over there," because, simply, sports fans in Tanzania are not the same as sports fans in Papua, New Guinea. Naturally, in each nation the fans frequently reflect their own national characteristics. The Italian fans are volatile, highly loyal, use their hands a lot. Japanese fans are modest, reserved. They will sit at a baseball game and politely applaud the umpires. Russian fans appear to be very well organized, do things in unison, and seem to have come off an assembly line. No one Russian fan will go against the grain during a game. Fans from the new African nations tend to be highly nationalistic, seeing each victory as a triumph for the country, a step upward.

Although they vary from country to country, there are certain characteristics that do group them together and separate them from us. The major difference is their choice of sports. Throughout almost all the rest of the world, the most watched, the most important, the most involving sport is soccer—uh, football.

Soccer is not just a sport in the rest of the world, it is a way of life. Everyone plays it, or has played it at one time or another. There are teams at every level of competition, from factory teams up through junior teams to professional and national amateur and national professional teams.

When a soccer team wins or loses, it is not a trifling matter. Bill Shankly, the manager of Liverpool's defending champions in the English Soccer League, understands the situation perfectly. "The way some people talk about modern football, anyone would think the results of just one game was a matter of life and death," he says. "They don't understand. It's much more serious than that."

It was much more serious to the townspeople of Catanzaro, a village in the south of Italy. On this Sunday morning the townspeople all went to church. By the afternoon they had all found enough strength to chase one referee all the way to Rome.

182 GOD SAVE THE PLAYERS

The Catanzaro team had just tied with visiting Palermo 1–1. The Catanzaro fans—which meant everyone living in Catanzaro—believed that their team should have been awarded two penalty kicks. Almost the entire town wanted to tell referee Vittorio Benedetti, who had come down from Rome to work the game, about the kicks.

As soon as the game ended, the fans began rioting. They chased Benedetti across the town and into a private house where he tried to find sanctuary. They tried to storm the house, to huff and puff and blow it down. They all gathered round, and so did the local police. The police encircled the house and tried to keep the mob away. Before long, eight policemen and one fan were injured in one or another of the interminable series of melees. The police prevailed, after an hour and with the help of a series of gas grenades. After the police rescued Benedetti, they escorted him all the way to Rome.

In Cosenza, Italy, the referee had to be helped from a soccer game he was working when he was hit in the groin by a transistor radio thrown by a fan. Police protection for the referee was somewhat better in Catania, Sicily, so the fans set fire to the stands after a penalty was awarded to the visiting team.

Life in Italian soccer is like that. But it's not just Italy, not just the emotional, outgoing Italian fans. There have been minor and major riots throughout Europe and South America over soccer. In Maracaibo Stadium in Rio de Janeiro, the largest stadium in the world—it holds close to 200,000 fans—a moat was built around the field to keep fans off. Actually, it didn't work particularly well. It just meant that the angry, emotional people chasing the other team and the referee are now wet, angry and emotional.

In Vigo, Spain, the mayor of the town—who

was also a very staunch hometown fan—fined a referee 10,000 pesetas for his "action and behavior" during a recent game. Vigo had lost the game.

Even the allegedly reserved, dignified British are not immune. Crowd excitement caused the death of 66 and an additional 145 injuries at one soccer match in Glasgow, Scotland, in 1971. The game was between archrivals Glasgow Celtics and Glasgow Rangers. This is something like Oklahoma versus Texas in football, the old Dodgers versus the old Giants in baseball and the Allies versus the Axis in war. All combined. Eighty thousand people were watching the game, which the Rangers were losing 1–0. As the game was nearly over, thousands of Ranger fans began rushing to the exits, trying to avoid the crowds. A group of Ranger fans then heard that their team had just tied the game, so they started back in. Soon, 40,000 people were pushing to get out and 40,000 were pushing to get back in. A steel barrier collapsed under the pushing, shoving weight of the crowd and 66 were dead.

The Glasgow Ranger fans are renowned all through Europe. A few seasons ago, Glasgow and thousands of their fans journeyed to Barcelona, Spain, to play Moscow Dynamo, for the European Cupwinners Cup, a very prestigious soccer event. Glasgow won, but the fans were not satisfied. When the game ended, several hundred Ranger supporters broke open liquor bottles and tossed them and tossed them. That was, of course, after they drank them and drank them. The fans threw the bottles at opposing players, at the referee, at the police. A police spokesman commented that "these people are animals." The soccer powers-that-be were just as impressed. The Rangers were suspended from European postseason tournament play for a year.

184 GOD SAVE THE PLAYERS

Fans recently have been getting so out of hand in the British Isles that the president of the English Soccer League and a member of Parliament have both advocated the birching of "spectators who indulge in violence." That means they want them whipped. "More ruthless action is imperative," said Len Shipman, the head of the league. "And I hope it will be taken on the government's direction. Fines will not stop the violence. The time has come for the return of the birch."

Soccer is not an excessively violent game, at least not when compared to our football and hockey. Yet it seems to create much more violence among its adherents than do our sports. In an important European Cup match in Munich in 1972, a fan threw an unopened Coca-Cola can, hitting an Italian player on the back of the head. The player was carried off on a stretcher, and before long the Italian team, dodging imaginary bottles and concentrating on the fans rather than on the German team, was behind 7–1. In frustration, one Italian player kicked the referee, and some more bottles rained down. The Italians lost. But since the conduct of European fans is so well known and such a factor in the result of games, the Italians decided to contest the result. They appealed to the Federation Internationale de Football association, the ruling body of the sport, charging that they were intimidated by the fans. The Federation upheld the appeal. The game was replayed—and the Italians won—on neutral grounds.

Not all the violence attributed to soccer fans is so public and engaged in by such large numbers. The fans can be just as violent in small numbers and away from the stadiums. In December 1973 a shot was fired into the home of Pelé. This was perhaps the most shocking episode of fan violence in recent years. Pelé, the black pearl of Brazil, is not just a soccer player; he is considered by many to be the greatest soccer player of all time. He is the highest-paid athlete in the world. He is considered a national resource by the Brazilian government. To shoot at him is something like lighting the fire in the fireplace on Christmas Eve.

Police believed that fanatical supporters of teams Pelé played against were responsible. Pelé, a forgiving sort, held nothing against them. The bullet, which smashed into his trophy case, did little damage. And anyway, a week earlier a bomb had exploded in his garden.

If Pelé can be attacked, is nothing sacred? Well, the marital vows surely are not. "Maria," a Peruvian housewife, wrote a letter to the lovelorn column of a Lima newspaper, complaining that her husband beat her every time Peru's soccer team lost a game. Not only that, but "I get a blow for every goal by which they lose. Chile beat Peru last Sunday and my husband came home like a madman. He hit me twice to make up for the two goals Chile won by." On the bright side, Maria was lucky her husband wasn't a pro-basketball fan.

Perhaps the major reason why soccer seems to provoke so much violence in its fans is its appeal to nationalism. In the United States, sports fanaticism is generally on a local basis. Affinity is based on where you live, which franchise you are closest to. There is local chauvinism involved, naturally, but how much passion can you put into an argument about the relative merits of Kansas City versus Milwaukee? And in a nation of transients, this week's Kansas City fan may be next week's Milwaukee fan.

But in the rest of the world, teams don't just represent a city or an area. They have those teams, too, but the most important teams are the national ones. They represent a whole nation —its manners, its political system, its language and its history. When you root for your national team, you are rooting for your way of life, for the superiority of your ethnic background. You are not just rooting for "bragging rights" to a city. You are rooting for national pride.

It was never more obvious than in 1969, in Central America. Honduras and El Salvador are two nations without much impact on the world. They are neither centers of finance, nor culture, nor war materiél. For these two countries, sports is their way to claim a national identity. And for these two countries, soccer *is* sport.

The two nations, adjacent to each other, were competing with each other in a series of soccer matches to determine qualifiers for the World Cup, the most prestigious trophy in all soccer. There had been bad blood between the two countries for a long time, stemming from differences over trade, economic problems and over the steady flow of Salvadorians into Honduras. The Salvadorians were taking jobs away from the Hondurans. The Hondurans were jealous of El Salvador's superior industrialization. El Salvador, a country one-quarter the size of Honduras, was envious of her neighbor's larger land and smaller population.

That was the background as the two national teams met in their best two-of-three series to determine the World Cup qualifier. The first game was played in Honduras and the home team won, 1–0. Rioting immediately followed. Honduran crowds moving out from the stadium began attacking all the Salvadorians they could find, eventually forcing at least 10,000 of them to leave the country.

The second game was played in El Salvador,

and the home team won this one, too, 3–0. Rioting immediately followed. The Honduran team itself was set upon and assaulted by hundreds of Salvadorians.

In an attempt to avoid additional riots, the third game of the series was scheduled for neutral ground, Mexico City. But by then it was too late. Within a week after the second game, the two nations broke off relations with each other. Within two more weeks Honduran authorities reported that Salvadorian troops had crossed the border and that Salvadorian planes had bombed Honduran cities. The war that would be called the "Soccer War" was on.

It didn't last very long, and the damage in life and property was not that great in a nuclear world. After two or three days the initially fierce fighting seemed to abate, mainly because both nations lacked war materiél. But some hostilities continued to simmer for months until the Organization of American States was able to gain a cease-fire.

The Soccer War was over then, but the nationalism that had flared in the arena of sport wasn't. The next time the teams from the two countries met, there was still another riot.

Nationalism seems particularly prevalent among sports fans in nations that are governed by dictatorships. To not be a fan of the national teams in those countries is almost a flagrant abuse of the party line. The team is us. And further, it shows the rest of the world that communism or monarchy or military fascism is the correct way.

When the United States Davis Cup team went to Rumania to play the challenge round, every time Americans Stan Smith or Tom Gorman served, all the Rumanians in Bucharest made sure to clear their throats simultaneously.

During the Olympics the officials of judgment sports seemed to be the most fanatical fans of all. If a Russian was boxing, the Russian judges voted for him. If an East German was ice skating, the East German officials scored for him. If a Spaniard was diving, the Spanish officials scored for him.

But it is perhaps in the Soviet Union and the People's Republic of China, the two largest non-democratic nations in the world, where sports and nationalism and politics become most thoroughly interwoven. Sport has always been approached in the Soviet Union as a national undertaking. Sports—winning—was something the entire country geared for. Winning games was something that could be dealt with in five-year plans. When the Russians decided to enter the Olympics in 1952, they set up "athletic factories" where top-level athletes were turned out one after another until the Russians dominated the Olympics.

When Valery Borzov, the sprinter, and Olga Korbut, the gymnast, disappointed in their performances the year after the last Olympics, they were excoriated in the Russian press. They were no longer, it was written, "bringing honor to the Soviet people." After Boris Spassky lost his world chess championship to Bobby Fischer, he became almost a pariah. His financial stipend was greatly reduced, he was not allowed out of the country to participate in many international tournaments. He was shunned in the newspapers and by many acquaintances. Not only had he lost, he had lost to a self-indulgent, money-mad American. His loss was a defeat for communism.

Politics took an even more activist role in the world of sports fans in Russia during the 1973 World University Games. The games were held in Moscow, and the Russians tried to keep everything on as professional a level as possible, since they wished to impress the rest of the world enough to be the host for the 1980 Olympics. Still, politics is politics.

The games took place during a period of great tension concerning Israel, Jews, internal dissent and Jewish emigration. Israeli athletes at the games became the focus of the tension. In apparently inspired demonstrations, Soviet spectators whistled and jeered at Israeli competitors as Russian Jews rallied to their support.

The situation exploded when a group of unidentified Russians physically attacked a group of Soviet Jews who had rooted for the Israeli basketball team. During the game, uniformed Soviet soldiers ripped up an Israeli flag held by Jewish fans, and other Russian spectators whistled and stomped their feet to show disapproval of the Israeli players.

The Russians are not much easier on fans from other countries. During the fall of 1972 the Soviet national hockey team and an all-star team from the National Hockey League played an eight-game series for supremacy of the ice. It was an unprecedented match, long in coming and highly emotional. For both the Soviet Union and Canada, winning the series was a matter of national pride. Both countries prided themselves on having the best hockey players in the world. Both groups of fans were highly motivated, but they showed their enthusiasm quite differently.

The Canadians were exuberant, loud, animated. They clapped rhythmically. They jumped up and down when something exciting happened on the ice. They did that for the four games in Canada and they tried to do that for the four games in the Soviet Union.

But for the contingent of Canadians who came to root their team on in Moscow, the reception was a little bit different. There was no organ to urge them on. Bob Woolf, the sports attorney, tells a story about what happened to one exuberant Canadian fan in Moscow.

"You know in Russia," Woolf says, "the fans are really frightened. They're frightened of the police and of the authorities. You can see it in their faces and in their behavior. You know, at first they weren't even cheering. They were just sitting there. Then they saw the Canadians doing it and so they picked it up a little.

"Anyway, it was the seventh game and a Canadian fan was feeling pretty good about things and he blew a horn, one of those air horns, during the game. He was immediately arrested for drunkenness. He was put under a cold shower for eight hours. All the hair was shaved off his head completely. They tattooed the bottom of both of his heels to indicate that he was arrested in the Soviet Union, which will be with him the rest of his life. He was sentenced to forty-five days in jail and was fined $280. And nobody could get him out. What do you think would've happened if a Russian had done it?"

In the other great communist nation of the world, the question would have never come up. In the People's Republic of China, fans would just not have done something like that. Winning is not that important in the land of Mao. According to the thought of the chairman, none are spectators, all are participants, and the purpose of sport is to further the revolution. With that as the purpose of sport, winning and losing must recede into the background. And if winning and losing are no longer important, it makes it very difficult to root. If you can't root for someone to win, or against someone, then it is exceedingly difficult to be a fan. A fan is someone who has almost a personal stake in a game's outcome. In China, there are no personal stakes.

Two *Sports Illustrated* reporters took a sports-oriented tour through China in 1973 and reported that in all the schools and universities they visited, they had never seen a single sports trophy or pennant. They asked a coach at a middle-level school where their trophies were kept. He told them: "It is true that sometimes we are awarded modest banners for winning, but I do not know where they are. Perhaps in a desk drawer. We consider friendship first, learning good technique second, victory banners third or even less."

"Don't your teams care if they win?" the reporters asked a Chinese interpreter. "Not so much," he said. "Our philosophy of sport is friendship first, competition second, you know. There is something to be learned from winning, but there is much to be learned from losing, also. We feel that the final score of a game is a matter of interest for a few moments, while the friendships developed go on for years, many years." Gradually the reporters learned that "sports victories in China are not only not celebrated much publicly, but that they are almost a matter of embarrassment."

Chuang Tse-Tung, the world champion table-tennis player during the late Sixties, was feared murdered during the cultural revolution, because, it was said, he had developed his own "cult of personality." Only one "cult of personality" to a country.

When an American all-star basketball team toured the People's Republic, Chinese spectators would sit watching them and remain almost funereally quiet. They never booed, never whistled, never rose to their feet. If they were impressed by a particular play, a low murmur might be heard. Most of the time they just applauded politely.

When the American table-tennis team opened the door to the previously forbidden country of the forbidden city, the Chinese team, vastly superior, almost always threw a game in each match. Winning was not that important.

Joe Namath could not sell shaving cream in the People's Republic of China. Fan clubs could not be started in the People's Republic. Beer cans could not be thrown at Pete Rose in the People's Republic.

The gap between sports fans in the People's Republic and in the republic of the United States seems massive, much wider than halfway around the world. And yet, when a table-tennis player hits a tremendous forehand smash, the Chinese are moved, impressed, just like the Americans would be. When a young Chinese girl throws the grenade—which is an official Chinese sporting event—farther than she ever did before, her friends and relatives are just as proud as the friends and relatives of an American girl who has just won her junior group swimming title.

It is different over there. It is different at a French boxing match where the fighters come in and everyone becomes very quiet instead of shouting "kill him." It is different at a skiing race in Switzerland, when the people ring cowbells to outline the route for their favorite skiiers. It is different in Brazil, where they explode firecrackers for the winner of a New Year's Eve road race. It is different in the Union of South Africa, where blacks cannot be fans of whites, and whites don't want to be fans of blacks.

The modes of expression, the levels of intensity, of feeling, are different. The *fact* of feeling is the same. There is caring, wherever the stadium. They can't legislate caring. Or against it.

THE QUESTION IS WHY
15

In this psychological phantasmagoria we search for a style, a way of ordering our existence, that will fit our particular temperament and circumstances. We look for heroes or mini-heroes to emulate. . . . Often we are unaware of the moment we commit ourselves to one life-style model over all others . . . for style of life involves not merely the external forms of behavior, but the values implicit in that behavior. . . .

—Future Shock, by *Alvin Toffler*

Why does Loudy Loudenslager panel his walls in Baltimore Colt jerseys? Why did Chris Drago decide against "saving the world"? Why do Alex and Bill sit quietly in the stands, oblivious to the world? Where does Richard Nixon get all those phone numbers?

Why does the man who doesn't like to go out in the warm spring rain to get a newspaper sit for three hours in a ten-degrees-below-zero blizzard watching a football game?

Why does a working stiff, who's having trouble getting his kids through school, shell out $100 for a seat—*one* seat—to watch two men in short pants pound their fists into each other?

Why did Marianne Moore, the poet, decide to write a poem to Roy Campanella and Pee Wee Reese? Why did Tiny Tim, the singer and husband of Miss Vicky, say that the greatest ambition in his life was to meet Gordie Howe, the hockey player? Why do thousands of people who've never been to South Bend, Indiana, who've never been to any college, consider themselves "subway alumni" of Notre Dame University?

194 GOD SAVE THE PLAYERS

In other words, why are these people fans? What makes them like this?

The answer to the questions are varied, tentative, sometimes contradictory. They reflect the perspectives of the answerers—that is, they are limited, biased, tunnel-visioned, sometimes self-congratulatory. They almost all miss the forest for the trees.

The marketing people, for example, explain the mania for sports in terms of selling the product. Through careful packaging, they have made sports fashionable, they say. Don Ruck, the vice-president of the National Hockey League, in charge of marketing, talks about selling sports to the public the way a used-car salesman talks about getting rid of the pink Edsel in the lot. "Chrysler," Ruck says, "might feel if they can put you behind the wheel, the car will sell you. Well, the way we feel is if we can put you into a seat for five games, then you're hooked. We just want to put you behind our wheel." To the marketers, the focus is the product.

To the sociologists, like Alvin Toffler, the focus is society. The sociologists use phrases like "leisure time," "disposable income," "voyeuristic society." Their theory is that sports fills gaps in society, that the need for sports reflects economic, cultural, even industrial trends in the world. There is so much free time, they theorize, the world is so large, so complicated, so distended, that we must have something to hold onto. As we become more and more alienated from physical tasks, we have started to gravitate more and more toward the exaltation of those who perform physical tasks for us.

The communications people attribute it all to "exposure." This is a theory that works hand-in-wallet with the theory of the marketing people. If you put it—football, the roller derby, goldfish fishing—on television, or in the papers or the magazines, you can't escape it. That damn game is always there. And it becomes part of your life.

Even taken all together these seem to be only surface explanations. There has to be something deeper. When Chris Drago follows Henry Aaron around for a year, sociology is not sufficient. When Detroit Shirley checks off another team, or league, it goes further than marketing analyses. When an entire borough, like Brooklyn, can find solace for its urban woes in the accomplishments of a baseball team, there are curious, deep-rooted factors at work.

This is, then, a question for the psychologists and psychiatrists. They are the ones who give us the reasons why our marriages don't work, why we make war, how we make love. They are the ones who try to explain us to ourselves.

Even the athletes themselves understand that this whole fan thing is a matter best left to them. As Sonny Jurgensen, the professional quarterback, puts it: "Playing pro football, particularly from the quarterback position, is like holding group therapy for 50,000 people every week. They bring their problems and accumulated frustrations to the stadium. You win and you diminish these problems. You lose and you've magnified them."

Henry Kellerman is a psychologist and psychoanalyst in private practice in New York City. He is director of psychology internship at the Post Graduate Center for Mental Health. He is an adjunct professor in the doctoral psychology program at the New School for Social Research. He was the editor of the clinical division newsletter of the New York State Psychological Association. He is also a fan. "I'm a Knick fan, a Billy Martin fan, an ex-Yankee fan, a New York Giant fan, a Joe Namath fan, a Sandy Koufax fan, a Willie

Mays fan and a Gale Sayers fan. Maybe a few others too."

As both psychologist and fan, he is able to examine the questions of fanhood with involvement, but also with a degree of clinical detachment. As both analyst and analysand, when he speaks of being a fan he understands the ramifications of his behavior.

"Sports," says Dr. Kellerman, "is a perfectly logical symbol of expressions of particularized conflicts in society. That's true sociologically and psychologically. Sports is symbolic cult. It's an expression of the society."

The society we live in is huge and complicated, alienating and fast-moving. It puts premiums on tangible measures of success and militates against interpersonal contact. It is a society of jet lag and assembly lines and two cars in every parking space. It is a society based on automation. Before this century, there was generally no need for mass spectator sports. Before, people were participants, everyone was active. In the old days, if you had conflict you could take it out on the horse, the land, the women. With the new society, in a world where conflict must be internalized, there are few logical ways to express of our conflicts.

So we turn to sports, we become fans. "Being a fan," says Dr. Harry Gunn, a diagnostic psychologist in Chicago, "encourages you to express emotion—if you like, conflicts—about something. You're permitted to holler for a guy's head without feeling guilty. It's really a vicarious outlet for all our civilized tensions."

The major conflict being worked out, Dr. Kellerman says, is the one brought on by the achievement drive. The achievement drive is the drive to "be successful, make a lot of money, to do better than your neighbor, get famous, to be a Hollywood movie star, to be a great baseball player." We put premiums on overt signs of accomplishment, but "not many of us can really make a lot of money or get on television. And so the achievement drive is blocked. "It must go somewhere," Dr. Kellerman says. In this culture, it frequently goes to sports.

So you pack up your achievement drive, get in the car and drive to the ball park. What happens there, by the right-field line or the 50-yard line, is that "a strong achievement drive, or a strong ambition drive, if you want to call it that, gets played out vicariously and mostly unconsciously in the symbolic arena," Dr. Kellerman explains. "The sports arena provides fans with an opportunity to express a multitude of conflicts. That's why sports is so popular. Actually, if not quite to express them, to see things that people are working out in themselves symbolically expressed on the field."

Sport offers a wide variety of expressions. The fan looking to work out his conflicts can find the perfect symbolization somewhere. Dr. Arnold R. Beisser, a clinical professor of psychiatry and human behavior at the University of California and the author of *The Madness in Sports*, explains that "in his fantasy, the fan can take any part that suits his psychic need. He may be the haughty favorite or the downtrodden underdog. He can project onto the players the whole gamut of his emotions as they enact the competitive drama."

Dr. Kellerman believes there is some empirical evidence for this thesis of projection. "Most women are not sports fans," he says, "while many men——you could almost say most men—— are. What I think this has to do with——and this is sort of confirmed by a lot of women's lib literature now——is that women are brought up not to have developed a sense of achievement but to think of encouraging the husbands to achieve, brothers to achieve, the men they know to achieve. The basic achievement drive in women never gets complicated and it never grows, the way the achievement drive for men grows. Consequently, they can satisfy what achievement drives they have much more easily, or they'll have their drives worked out by somebody else, the men. So they don't need to work it out through sports events."

To the fans, of course, it is not projection, not symbolic. It is real, palpably real. "From the stands, people seem to feel excitement or depressions, depending on the fortunes of their team," says Dr. Burton Siegal, a psychiatrist from Hinsdale, Illinois. "It's as though they themselves have won or lost something."

At the games the fans can feel they've won or lost, something they can't do quite as easily in life. The world is fraught with ambiguities. Sports offers something definite, something solid. Unlike the all-too-real world, sports is a world divided into black and white, offense and defense, hits and errors. It is a world with a defined beginning, middle and end. And it is a world that offers up a result, an actual decision. There are winners and losers, right and wrong in sports. You don't win or lose—or even tie—as a mailman or poet. You can't measure your accomplishment as a secretary or a furrier by what's up there on the scoreboard.

There is a scoreboard for everyone at the stadium, and it is a scoreboard everyone can read and understand and discuss. We are all in tune, sitting in section 21, and that is an important factor, too. Because not only do fans project onto the field, they also project onto the rest of the fans.

The society is diffused and so we don't make

connections. We live cut off from each other. Where else can we join in common pursuit, feel bonds?

"Everyone needs to feel he has ties with others," Dr. Beisser says. "In today's complex society, family ties have become attenuated and clan ties have all but disappeared. Grown children rarely continue to live in the same town as their parents. Often they leave the social class in which they were born. Leaving behind one's roots makes it difficult to have a clear picture of one's place in the present and its relationship to the past and future. The greater the disruption, the greater becomes the individual's need for something with which to identify.

"With the dispersal of the traditional extended family, the clan, and the tribe, this need to be identified with a group of some kind becomes more intense. The fan can get to know the team as well as he knows his own family. In effect, by doing all the things a fan does, he becomes a member of a larger, stronger family group, a collective entity comparable in some sense to the tribe and the clan.

"The fan also enjoys a peculiarly luxurious position between the camaraderie and the anonymity of the crowd. He can have intense feelings with strangers who understand."

"We want to feel something in common with other people," Dr. Kellerman says. "We want to be part of something larger than ourselves, but at the same time don't wish to make any long-term commitments."

So we commit ourselves to a crowd, to a team or a player. We choose the Houston Oilers or the Cleveland Cavaliers or Bobby Hull or Willie Stargell. We use this team or that player to work out the drives that have been blocked by a society that prizes control. We choose that team or this player because they fulfill needs that are no longer satisfied by lover or family or community. But why is it *this* player and *that* team? Why this sport and not the other one? Why, say, a congenital loser instead of an assured winner?

"Each individual's particular psychological makeup will determine what sport, or team, or individual he favors," says Dr. Kellerman. It depends on what particular conflicts the fan is trying to work out. "A good example of something like that is when the Knicks played the Lakers in the NBA play-offs in 1970. The Knicks embodied the ideals of teamwork, five individuals bending together for the common good, everyone subordinating their natural instincts. While the Lakers, with Chamberlain and West, were the perfect example of the star system. Everyone did not take part; everyone's job and importance was not equal.

"Now, most achievement drives are concerned with success and money, which are sort of vacuous goals. Somewhere in the personality of people who have those kinds of drives is basically the idea of being your brother's keeper, of not being so competitive. Those are the people who would have rooted for the Knicks. Because with the Knicks you could have your achievement drive satisfied without being singled out. In other words, you could still be very competitive and also be involved in a cooperative endeavor. Since man is basically a flock animal, he would rather be involved in the cooperative effort. So if you root for the Knicks you can be rewarded for being better than the others, but within our social structure.

"Now, those who rooted for the Lakers wanted to be competitive, but did not want to do it within our social structure. They were generally people who couldn't deal with other people, who were introverts, loners. They were people who did not want to help, or to be helped. Of course, all of this is talking in a vacuum. If you happened to live in Los Angeles and you were the most cooperative of people, you probably still rooted for the Lakers."

That's assuming you chose basketball in the first place. You might have chosen football or baseball or hockey. Rather than a noncontact sport, you might have chosen a violent one. That is the choice more fans seem to be making now.

"It's a violent time," says Dr. Milton Reisner, director of psychiatry for the Westchester County (New York) Mental Health Board. "Sports becomes a safety valve for that violence. When the police want to stop gang fights they try to steer the kids into competitive sports—the Police Athletic League, for instance—to drain a little aggressive energy. If not for sports like football and hockey, it might be a much more violent time. With all the violence we are subjected to, the capacity for violence is built up in ourselves. I think there'd be a tremendous number of fights in the stands if you didn't know the police would come and the other guy would sue you. The way we are taught, if you're going to punch somebody in the nose and you don't enjoy it, there's something wrong with you. Assuming, of course, that you have a good reason to punch somebody in the nose. What it comes down to is that it's the behavior of the players that's tapping the fans' unconscious drives."

Fraser Kent, a doctor and the medical writer for the *Miami Herald*, sees football fans as some sort of bloodsucking parasites. "The greatest excitement in football," he writes, "appears to be directly related to the potential for, or the probability of, serious injury."

It is not just the violence, the threat of imminent injury, which causes the fan to choose, say, football over baseball. It is, once again, those old particularized conflicts the fan's always carrying around.

"Take football," Dr. Kellerman explains. "If someone is highly involved in achievement and ambition drives and very successful, or highly involved and very frustrated with it, but the energy is still percolating about that, then football provides an excellent opportunity for that to be expressed. That's because in football, everything is highly competitive. It's really acute competitiveness. It's not like you can make 40 errors, like a third baseman in baseball. If you make two errors, you won't be playing. Each play means more, each game means more. If a quarterback, even a Joe Namath, can't move his team for two quarters, then he won't be there for the third quarter. That acute competitiveness is the major attraction for people who are always involved in highly competitive situations."

This is a theory which seems to be borne out by the survey the National Football League made of its fans which stated that "52% of our fans are professional, management and executive types"—people involved in highly competitive situations.

Statistically, that is not the makeup of the usual baseball fan. The psychological makeup is different, too. In baseball, the behavior of the players is much less violent, more self-contained. Baseball is a bucolic, almost placid game. The acute competitiveness isn't there, and so the type of fan is not usually highly competitive.

"Children are baseball fans," Dr. Kellerman claims, "children and the type of person who is still very much a child. I would say that by and large—and this is a wild claim and I have nothing to back it up—I would say that the average score on a maturity test for baseball fans is probably lower than for football or basketball fans. Baseball, although a team sport, requires less coordination with the other members of the team. Essentially, it is perceived as an individual team sport. People who are not involved in cooperative efforts, then, would tend more to baseball. If you're dealing in a competitive framework, you must deal with other people. Baseball doesn't provide that framework. The synchronization that is required in football is not required in baseball. Football also requires subordination and self-control, and those are the qualities that require somewhat more maturity."

So, together with your achievement drive and assorted psychological needs, you've chosen your sport. If you're highly competitive, frustrated, if the violence has built up within, you've probably chosen a highly competitive, violence-prone sport or team. You want to see your conflicts worked out. Winning—the game, the fight, the pennant—will do that for you. But then why would you choose a chronically losing team? Why would a fan choose as his symbolic partner a third-string halfback or a reserve shortstop? Why do some fans seem to get such inordinate pleasure out of being beaten? Why did so many people become fans of the early New York Mets, one of the worst baseball teams ever to trip over home plate, but also one of the most lavishly supported?

"It's a very complicated question," Dr. Kellerman answers. "But one of the things we could say is that people would choose the Mets if they were a *sure* loser, which they just about were. That's because the only way some people can become motivated in their lives is if they're basically up against the wall. Then they get motivated. It's a certain kind of person with that kind of conflict. It would be natural for that type of person to choose a team, or a player, that had its back up against the wall. Then he could root for the Mets, or whomever, to overcome whatever obstacles are in their way. Okay, the Mets don't win. But they *could*. Eventually, they'll win one game. Or the terrible hitter will hit one home run.

"The person who feels he must have his back to the wall to become motivated keeps getting himself into a situation where his back is to the wall time and time again, a situation where he must overcome great obstacles. This presumably convinces him that he's not really inadequate. That he can conquer anything. He needs to convince himself that he can do it. However, he never really convinces himself and that's why he has to do it over and over again, starting from zero. That's what's known as the repetition-compulsion conflict.

"Then there's the individual who has never really resolved all the conflicts in his subconscious. He's essentially remained in the role of the child in his relations to other people in the world who have become the adults. He must be identified, or associated, or affiliated with a circumstance that confirms that to him, that he's a child. Which means a loser. He's more comfortable in that role."

In any discussion of psychological conflicts and motivation, sex, naturally, becomes involved. It must, said Dr. Freud. And it does, says Detroit Shirley.

"Aggression and sex are the two major drives in man," says Dr. Reisner. "So of course in our sports we would look for and find sexual aspects."

There is, Dr. Reisner goes on, in certain sports a definite sexual attraction that brings out a certain type of fan. Boxing seems to be a very good example.

Dr. Kellerman believes that sex (actually, he calls it "erotic aspects") is why a large percentage of women seem to be attracted to boxing. Although most women are not sports fans, sports like boxing, hockey, the roller derby and wrestling seem to be more attractive to them than are the more sedate sports. "When you're watching two strong, muscular men, there has to be some eroticism and physicality involved in the reason why you're watching," he says. "There have to be some erotic, vicarious fantasies played out about that. Also, the woman has the opportunity there to be the child and the mother. You have a man in short pants, and you can be the mother. And here is the strong man, and you are the child. The woman can be both the overpowered one and the overpowering one. And when you deal with fantasies of being overpowered, you are dealing with sex."

The question that psychologists—and sociologists and everybody else—must ask themselves is: Is all this rooting good? Is being a fan something useful, beneficial, good for the individual, good for the society? Or is it destructive? Is it a smoke screen? Rather than helping to solve problems, does it instead prevent us from coming to grips with the problems? Perhaps, even worse, is *it* the problem itself?

Most psychoanalysts accept the concept of fandom and believe it is, in some sense, useful. "When people are at a game and yell, 'kill him,' they really mean it," says Dr. Reisner. "Of course, they wouldn't really kill him themselves, but the game provides an outlet, a safe outlet."

If not for these safe outlets, many psychiatrists feel, the frustrations would go somewhere else, someplace much more dangerous than a sports stadium. They believe we must recognize the fact that those frustrations and aggressions are not going to go away by themselves. People *are* aggressive, people *are* driven, people do need community, and this is as good a way as any other—perhaps better—to fulfill those needs.

"For modern man," says Dr. Beisser, "regression, the return to simpler and more elemental stages of adjustment, is acceptable within the matrix of sports watching. Regression, if controlled, tends to refurbish the individual for return to the monotony of daily life."

Dr. Gunn of Chicago feels that being a fan has "therapeutic benefits. We see the qualities of strength, courage, daring and ability in sports that we all like to identify with. Sports encourages you to express emotion about something, while during the rest of your life you're not generally permitted to express any kind of emotion." Dr. Gunn then resurrects the familiar phrase: Being a fan, he says, "is a useful outlet."

In essence, most psychoanalysts feel that sports can and has served as the nation's largest free-floating encounter group. And that's good, because anything that brings us in touch with our buried emotions is good.

But the verdict is not unanimous. Dr. Kellerman, for one, disagrees, and on the most elemental point: Being a fan, being interested in sports, is not a "safe" outlet. In fact, he claims, it it is not an outlet at all.

"People who are fans keep rooting for the same thing day in and day out," he says. "Each game they want the same thing to happen. That's because on a symbolic level they can't work anything out at all. They never work anything through. If the conflict on a reality level remains in your life, then you can root for something symbolic over and over again. All it tends to do is to relieve your anxiety in your fantasy life. I guess that's good. But in reality, the conflict remains. So what rooting for a team does, it seems to me, is to diffuse the energies you have from dealing with the reality level.

"If the conflict is resolved in reality, you don't need to be a fan anymore. The symbolic isn't necessary for you to act out your needs. To put it another way, sports can be cathartic, but never therapeutic."

Dr. Kellerman blames the society as much as the individual for refusing to deal on the reality level. "When society deals with more substantive issues and less superficial ones, people will probably stop being fans, at least fans as we know the term. Because when the society moves away from the superficial, the elements of successful competition—money, fame and the like—will no longer be important. When we move away from competitiveness, people will be able to start dealing with reality. When they deal with reality, they won't need fantasy. Sports, as we know them now, wouldn't sustain itself."

Dr. Kellerman envisions a utopian world—he calls it a "humanist society"—where "some form of sport will develop that emphasizes cooperation, cooperation in the service of something else. In a humanistic society the people won't be infused with neurotic competitiveness. The achievement drive will not be the dominant factor it is now. The people won't *need* sports. They will be able to choose, in the psychological sense."

But in the meantime?

"In the meantime," says Dr. Kellerman, "in the meantime, I have to go and watch the Knick game now."

ON THE INSIDE
16

Primitive people made idols of wood and stone, civilized people make idols of flesh and bone.
—George Bernard Shaw

Most athletes are not fans. They never had the time.

They were too busy working on their passing or their base-stealing or their jump shots. The difficulties in becoming a professional athlete, a minority of a minority, are so immense that, to make it, there can be no distractions. The athlete usually must devote all his being to that one end. While others are discovering books and music, sequential calculus and the Paleolithic age, the aspiring athlete is honing his skills, advancing his game. If they were fans as kids, they lost it somewhere along the way to the major leagues.

From the time of the first Little League game, or the first choose-up in the schoolyard, the athlete was never on the outside, never looking on. He never developed the passivity that is necessary to be an accomplished fan. He was always *doing*, and so was always the focus, the object of attention. He never had the time or opportunity to develop the perspective of the spectator.

"A fan? I just wasn't. Never considered it. I didn't care to," says Jim Plunkett, the quarterback for the New England Patriots. "I only got one autograph in my entire life and that was when I was at a banquet and got in a line like everyone else did and then found that I had accidentally gotten in the autograph line."

"To me," says Larry Csonka of the Miami Dolphins, "the real reality is out there on the field. That's the reality between you and the other players."

Being a fan is something learned. It's cumulative, a piling on of learned responses, remembered games, unforgotten stimuli. It's not something you can just pick up.

Just like movie stars who don't attend movies, even their own, ballplayers rarely go to see ball games. If they do, it is for analytical purposes, or because there is nothing else to do, or because they can get in for nothing. When the athlete does go, he doesn't go to root, to jump up and down, to scream and berate and plead. That visceral excitement isn't there for him.

Bill Bradley, the professional basketball player, went to college about 60 miles from Madison Square Garden. It didn't matter. "I was in the Garden only once in my life before I played there," Bradley remembers. "I supposedly had a date with this Danish girl in New York when I was at Princeton. I took the bus to town. I waited for her and she never showed. I had nothing to do so I wandered over to the Garden, bought a ticket and sat in the balcony."

The athlete, so far removed, is also too close to be a fan. He knows that number 24 suffers from a severe case of body odor. Number 16, he's aware, had a little thing with a waitress and now with a paternity suit. How could he root for a runaway father?

He also knows the pain and the anguish other athletes go through, so how could he boo them? He knows that sport is a business, and these men performing in front of him are getting paid. He knows they are real people, not icons or evil spirits.

"I don't criticize," Jim Plunkett says. "I've

been in the same kind of situations and I know."

The athlete both knows too much and not enough. He never could, nor would he want to, assimilate the experiences that go into the making of a fan. To him the fan is something exotic, something strange, a manifestation so foreign it is almost inexplicable.

The athlete stands out there in the middle of Yankee Stadium or Chavez Ravine or Boston Garden or RFK Stadium and the faces and voices blend, become indistinguishable, a collective mass. The athlete who walks down the street or into a restaurant and is besieged for autographs has usually perfected the ability of signing or acknowledging without looking at the people. They become the autograph hunters, or the wavers, or the ones patting him on the back.

"You start dealing with them as a group, you don't think of them as individuals," says Ron Swoboda, the outfielder last employed by the Atlanta Braves. "You don't think of them as individuals, the same way they don't think of you as an individual. They're human beings, but at the park, particularly, they're just a mass. It's not good for you to deal with them individually."

Whether as a mass or individuals, the athlete still must deal with the fan. Most modern athletes have realized that. They understand they are public property and that their success, during and most especially after their athletic careers, is dependent on how well they get along with their public. So almost all are courteous, willing to sign, to pose, to stand and talk for a few minutes. It's part of the price they know they must pay. They have accustomed themselves to it, do it without much thought. Necessary evil is the term most of them use for the fan.

Of course, the athletes make distinctions among fans. Usually the distinctions are geographic. Almost all professionals have unkind words to say about the city of Philadelphia and the fans of Philadelphia. "Not only would they boo a funeral there," says Clete Boyer, the former baseball player, "but they might even throw bottles at the hearse. It must be the city. All they want to do is boo there."

Athletes in all sports are generally contemptuous of fans in California, considering them ignorant and not true fans. Detroit and Boston and sometimes New York get praise from athletes for having the most knowledgeable fans, while Chicago and Saint Louis fans are generally considered frontrunners. The athletes prefer fans who are vocal and active—"You don't want to play in a TV studio," they say—but they don't enjoy fans who are too vocal or too active. They draw the line.

The line can be a very distinct one for the athlete. John Havlicek, of the Boston Celtics, talks about eating in a restaurant, and the line he draws there. "If I've already started eating," he says, "I just won't sign autographs. But if they come over before I've started, I'll sign as many as I can. That's not really too much of an imposition. I'm used to that. But when I'm in the middle of my meal and they start to come over, I just politely tell them to wait until after I finish and I'll be glad to sign for them. Sometimes, some of them aren't too happy about that. That's when they start to get belligerent. You know, some guy will come over to me and say, 'Hey, Havlicek, you're not so tough. I could take you.' So I tell him, 'You're probably right. You can beat me up. Good-night.' What else can you say?"

Havlicek, like most intelligent athletes, has nothing but good to say about fans—in general terms, that is. But when he talks of specific instances, he seems to remember only the unpleasant situations. "Like you're signing an autograph," he says, "and right after you finish, they'll tear it up right in your face. Or sometimes when there are a lot of them, they'll start tearing at your clothing. Or later you'll find that you have magic marker all over you. And you know that some do it intentionally.

"I remember this one guy at a function I attended. He came up to me very nicely and asked for an autograph. I said sure, and started giving it to him. Fine. After I gave it to him, the guy just had to say *something*. So he turns to me and says, 'Thank you, Mr. Cowens.'" Havlicek smiles. "You know, I really can't understand how people can do things like that."

Ron Swoboda thinks he understands. "I think that when you speak about fans you have to employ some of what the police department calls mob psychology. They are essentially a mob, even if there are only a few of them together in a bar. And each part of that mob tries to impress the other parts. That's why they do things that they almost undoubtedly wouldn't do alone. But I'll tell you, I don't know what they would do alone. I don't know what a fan is. I don't know if all by yourself, a person is a fan."

In Pittsburgh one season, Swoboda was being harassed by one fan, part of the right-field group of fans. The harassment went on throughout the game. It was obscene and vicious. Finally a foul ball was hit near the fan and Swoboda went over. He singled out the fan, splitting him from his mob, shearing him of his protection. Eyeball-to-eyeball. "Now, what do you have to say?" the ballplayer asked the fan.

For a moment, the fan was speechless. Finally: "Swoboda, you're my man."

Swoboda wasn't bitter or terribly angered when he confronted the man. More than anything else, he was curious. The athlete is so removed—in experience and background—from the fan that usually his only response is curiosity. Why? Why are they doing that?

"I remember the first time I was ever booed by a home crowd," Jim Plunkett is saying. "Throughout my entire career, in Little League, high school, college, I had never been booed by the home crowd. Then suddenly I was being booed, and shouted at, and people were yelling from the stands and calling me all sorts of names. I was shocked. I knew I hadn't been playing very well and the team hadn't been winning, but I was shocked anyway. I couldn't really understand why they were doing it."

The boos cascade down, and the professional athlete, through years of training, manages to ignore it. Or so he says. "You try to ignore it, to block it out," says Plunkett, "but you're a human being, and you feel bad. I mean think of being rejected by fifty thousand people, all at once."

Not all athletes try or are able to ignore it. If they are being cheered by 49,999 fans, these players can hear the one softly chanting boo. The sensitive ones are said to have "rabbit ears." When you consider that Wilt Chamberlain is seven feet two inches tall, and has rabbit ears, those are pretty big ears.

Chamberlain has never been a favorite of the fans. It is perhaps the price he must pay for being the top dog in a nation of underdog-lovers. The fact that he has not been totally successful in his career has added to the fans' treatment of him, and also to his resentment. "American fans are spoiled," Chamberlain believes. "They only care about winning. They just can't give credit to a team for getting this far." This was said just after Chamberlain's team had lost again, in the final round of the National Basketball Association play-offs. "They just can't enjoy great games between great teams. They don't realize that one of them has to lose. They don't realize it's how you play that counts, not whether you win. They treat losers like animals. In fact, they're animals."

Chamberlain's perspective is, generally, a minority one. But other athletes also feel that fans are intolerant. "They show the same lack of tolerance that sportswriters do," says Stan Love, a basketball player now with the Los Angeles Lakers. "I'm considered a flake so the fans always yell at me—especially when I had a beard during my rookie year. The fans want ballplayers to fit their own idea of what a ballplayer should be, and they certainly don't want freaks on their team. They won't let you be yourself, what you want to be."

Derek Sanderson, maybe the flakiest, freakiest athlete in America, has gone on being himself no matter what the fans have told him they wanted. Sanderson, who has also occasionally called fans "animals," believes that "you really can be anything the fans want you to be. That's because no matter who you are, they're going to see you in their own perspective. I mean, to some of them I may be freaky. But I bet to some others I'm the straightest cat in the world. Sports fans are a whole subculture. They have their own standards. Man, it just doesn't pay to listen to them. You just gotta do your own thing."

Do your own thing. Sure. Let Richard Nixon decide to go to a porno flick. Let Paul Newman decide to go nude sunbathing at Coney Island. Let Billie Jean King decide to date Bobby Riggs. It just can't be done. They are public figures.

"Sometimes I feel like an amoeba on a slide," Phil Jackson of the New York Knicks says. "As an athlete," says John Havlicek, "you have no private life unless you isolate yourself. If I want to just go for a walk with my wife, or we just want to go to a neighborhood restaurant to get a bite, we can't. We know what it means."

"You're a celebrity, somebody special," says Ron Blomberg, occasional right fielder for the New York Yankees. "Everywhere you go, you look and you see people staring at you. That's great, it's a good feeling. It's great to have an image, to be somebody. But you got to carry that image around with you all the time. No matter where you go, you got to be Ron Blomberg, baseball player. You can't just be someone who wants to drink a couple of beers. Almost all fans are good people, real nice, but you just wish sometimes that they weren't fans and you weren't public property."

After he had lost to Sonny Liston in an embarrassingly short period of time, Floyd Patterson decided he didn't want to be public property. To avoid the stares, he put on a false beard, glasses, an ill-fitting hat and slunk out of town. Most other athletes wouldn't go that far, because as much as they complain about the attention, they crave it. Wilt Chamberlain, who wishes that everybody would just leave him alone, built an extravagantly plush home on a Southern California hilltop and then invited the press to preview it. Joe Namath kept inviting press people up to his apartment so they could tell the rest of the world about his llama rug. Ballplayers in all sports have bought flamboyant cars and then added license plates with their initials or nicknames or team numbers.

Perhaps they crave attention because they know it will all soon be gone. They know that one of these seasons they're going to walk into a restaurant and no one is going to bother them, before, during or after they eat. They're going to be walking down a street and no one is going to wave. No more public property. Just another guy, just like everybody else.

"I remember this story I was told about this baseball player and his coach who were sitting somewhere in some lounge," Jim Plunkett recollects. "Everybody was trying to get the player's autograph and talk to him because he was very famous and one of the biggest stars in the game. And standing next to him is this coach, who was once a great baseball player, one of the best. And he's just sitting by, nobody talking to him. One of the fans gets the player's autograph and then walks over to the coach and says, 'And who did you used to be?'"

It is an image that haunts the professional athlete. For the first 30 years of their lives they usually cultivate nothing but their athletic skills. When the skills leave them, they are left with nothing. They are like parents who have devoted their lives to their children, sacrificing all. Then the children grow up, the parents are bereft, no interests and activities of their own. The athlete has never known the sound of no hands clapping.

They say they wish the fans wouldn't bother them, but when they stop, the silence is deafening to them. Cookie Gilchrist, a professional football player who ended his career in 1967, has started an organization called United Professional Athletics Coalition of America, Inc. It is sort of a decompression chamber for athletes who are getting back into civilian life. The group, Gilchrist says, will try to help the athlete make the adjustment by helping to restore the confidence that is taken away when the cheering stops. "It's the overall rejection by the same masses that once applauded, cheered, catered to, pampered, loved, hated these men," Gilchrist says. "All of a sudden one day you're walking down the street and nobody recognizes you. You go into a bank and try to borrow money and you can't. In a sense you've been used up. The fans have used you up."

During their careers the athletes thought it was the other way around; they thought they were using the fans. They did impose sometimes, asking for too many autographs, pulling at the new sports jacket, disturbing dinner. But they were okay. They had their place—in the stands—and the athletes had theirs.

It is only when the two intersect dramatically that the athlete becomes fully aware of the fan. And when that happens, well, the athlete isn't too thrilled with the whole thing.

Perhaps the truest picture of the athlete's attitude toward the fan is seen in the reaction of Mike Curtis, Baltimore Colts linebacker. In December 1971 Curtis was at his most public when his team was playing the Miami Dolphins in Baltimore. The fans, of course, were there, but they were on one side of the rail and Mr. Curtis was on the other. Perfect coexistence, Mr. Curtis felt.

Among those in the stands was Mr. Donald Ellis, 30 years old, of Rochester, New York. Mr. Ellis had been a normal if somewhat active fan throughout most of the game. Then, in the third period, Mr. Ellis was suddenly seized with an uncontrollable urge to vault the fence, run onto the field and grab the football, the one Mr. Curtis and friends were playing with.

"My friends didn't think I would do it," Mr. Ellis said later. "I didn't know I would do it either. But suddenly I was out there."

The Dolphins were huddling. The Colts were leisurely lined up by the ball, waiting for the play to start. And here comes this strange figure in a flopping overcoat. The figure runs out onto the field, stops and snatches the ball and then heads for the opposite sideline.

In true professional fashion, the Dolphins and

the Colts ignored the fan. If you just ignore them, eventually they'll go away, they felt. All except Mike Curtis.

Mr. Curtis raced for the interloper, much as if his dinner had been interrupted by an autograph seeker. He caught up with him and gave Mr. Ellis a brutal smash to the neck with a padded forearm. Mr. Ellis decided to stop running, and fell unconscious.

Later, Mr. Curtis explained why he had done such a thing. First he was somewhat objective: "I believe in law and order. That fellow had no right on the field. I felt it was in line to make him aware of his wrongdoing."

Then he became much more subjective: "I couldn't take the idea of people getting in my way when I was doing my job," the athlete said about the fan.

Mr. Ellis later decided to sue Mr. Curtis and the Baltimore Colts for $250,000. He was attacked, he claimed, "without provocation."

So the lines were drawn once again. The ballplayers have understood about those lines all along. The world, they know, is divided into two kinds of people: us and them, participants and spectators. It's destiny.

But what the ballplayers have not understood is that they are the minority. There are more of us. And our ranks are always increasing. We'll go on forever. It's destiny.

It was my destiny to sit in the stands with most men and acclaim others. It was my fate, my destiny, my end, to be a fan.
　　　　—*Frederick Exley, from* A Fan's Notes

ABOUT THE AUTHOR

Neil Offen is a fan. He is a fan of the New York Knicks, French Bordeaux, early 1950s horror movies, Bob Gibson, Hitchcock movies made in England, the Montreal Canadiens, out-of-the-way subterranean Italian restaurants, Waylon Jennings, Amsterdam, Bette Davis, Marty Liquori, late 1950s horror movies, Beaux Arts architecture, Brooks Robinson, James Joyce, the early Mamas and Papas, novels in urban settings, Paul Klee and Roger Staubach.

He managed to develop all these affinities while growing up in New York City, where he still lives with his wife who likes all those things except the early '50s horror movies. He is a former sportswriter for the *New York Post*, where he covered everything from roller derby to baseball and hockey. He has written articles for many major national magazines and is the co-author with Jim Bouton of the emotionally wrenching "*I Managed Good, But Boy Did They Play Bad.*" He doesn't like bad reviews.

OTHER SELECTIONS FROM PLAYBOY PRESS

HOW I WOULD PITCH TO BABE RUTH
Tom Seaver with Norman Lewis Smith
Seaver vs. the Sluggers—Babe Ruth, Joe DiMaggio, Hank Aaron, Roberto Clemente, Stan Musial, Ted Williams—plus John Updike on Ted Williams's last day, Murray Kempton on the autumn of Willie Mays's career, and Roger Kahn on two of the greatest boys of summer—Jackie Robinson and Gil Hodges. In all, a book rich in baseball lore and charged with the thought-provoking insights of one of baseball's most knowledgeable superstars.
$1.50

SUPER DETECTIVE
B. W. von Block
The many lives of Tom Ponzi, Europe's master investigator, whose cases ranged from daring thefts and high-level espionage to international drug traffic.
$1.25

MEN OF COURAGE
William Parker, ed.
20 gripping stories of real-life adventures, from bullfighting to mountain climbing.
$1.50

SOLO
Harry Roskolenko, ed.
This fascinating collection probes the psyches of 18 courageous adventurers as they tell in their own words what it takes to face the ultimate hazards of nature—alone.
$1.50

GREAT COURTROOM BATTLES
Richard E. Rubenstein, ed.
The most dramatic and exciting courtroom battles of our time, including the emotion-charged trials of Lizzie Borden, Al Capone, Alger Hiss, Billy Mitchell, Adolf Eichmann and Lieutenant Calley.
$1.50

PLAYBOY'S INVESTMENT GUIDE
Michael Laurence
Written by *Playboy*'s award-winning business and finance editor, this is the widely acclaimed guidebook to stock and bond markets, mutual funds, commodities and collector's items—every area where adventurous investors can reasonably expect profits.
$1.50

INSTANT MILLIONAIRES
Max Gunther
Exciting and provocative stories of 36 business geniuses who wanted to get rich quick—and succeeded. Plus 14 "uninvented inventions" that can lead to a fast fortune.
$1.50

CHIODO—UNDERCOVER COP
Charles Whited
The extraordinary but true story of a New York City undercover cop—more revealing than *Serpico* and more explosive than *Super Cops*.
$1.50

KEN PURDY'S BOOK OF AUTOMOBILES
The number-one book on cars and drivers by the number-one writer on motoring.
$1.95

HOW TO TALK DIRTY AND INFLUENCE PEOPLE
Lenny Bruce
The controversial comedian's own story, told in the style that made him famous.
$1.50

THE SUPER CROOKS
Roger M. Williams, ed.
The most flamboyant and clever hustlers, swindlers and thieves of England and America are captured here, including Moll Cutpurse, John Dillinger, Jesse James, Billie Sol Estes, the Brinks Robbers and Britain's Great Train Robbers.
$1.50

Order directly from:

Playboy Press
The Playboy Building
919 North Michigan Avenue
Chicago, Illinois 60611

No. of copies	Title	Price
____ C16259	How I Would Pitch to Babe Ruth	$1.50
____ B16222	Super Detective	$1.25
____ C16188	Men of Courage	$1.50
____ C16246	Solo	$1.50
____ C16233	Great Courtroom Battles	$1.50
____ C16254	Playboy's Investment Guide	$1.50
____ C16243	Instant Millionaires	$1.50
____ C16235	Chiodo—Undercover Cop	$1.50
____ E16216	Ken Purdy's Book of Automobiles	$1.95
____ C16241	How to Talk Dirty and Influence People	$1.50
____ C16242	The Super Crooks	$1.50

Please enclose 50¢ for postage and handling.

Total amount enclosed: $

Name _____

Address _____

City _____ State _____ Zip _____

WE HOPE YOU ENJOYED THIS BOOK.

IF YOU'D LIKE A FREE LIST OF OTHER PAPERBACKS AVAILABLE FROM PLAYBOY PRESS, JUST SEND YOUR REQUEST TO MARILYN ADAMS, PLAYBOY PRESS, 919 NORTH MICHIGAN AVENUE, CHICAGO, ILLINOIS 60611.